hrlg

JUN - - 2021

The
Avenging Angel

Center Point
Large Print

**This Large Print Book carries the
Seal of Approval of N.A.V.H.**

WEST OF THE BIG RIVER

The
Avenging Angel

*A Novel Based on
the Life of Orrin Porter Rockwell,
Religious Enforcer and
Deputy United States Marshal*

MICHAEL NEWTON

CENTER POINT LARGE PRINT
THORNDIKE, MAINE

This Center Point Large Print edition
is published in the year 2021 by arrangement with
Western Fictioneers.

The text of this Large Print edition is unabridged.
In other aspects, this book may vary
from the original edition.
Printed in the United States of America
on permanent paper.
Set in 16-point Times New Roman type.

ISBN: 978-1-64358-915-2

The Library of Congress has cataloged this record
under Library of Congress Control Number: 2021930331

CHAPTER 1

Utah Territory: March 1, 1858

Facing a bitter wind, his wide-brimmed hat pulled low and tied beneath his chin, long hair whipping away behind, the rider offered up a silent prayer of thanks as Salt Lake City rose before him from the trackless desert. He was cold and weary, feeling every one of his forty-four years and nine months, craving nothing so much as a hot meal and deep tub of water to match. His buckskin garb and heavy fleece-lined coat helped with the wind, but only to a point. His Appaloosa gelding bore the brunt of it without complaint, trailing a dead man draped across the saddle of a roan.

At least it wasn't snowing yet, and while the sharp wind off the Wasatch Mountains stung the rider's face, it kept the man he'd killed from going ripe too soon.

The dead man—Heber Skousen—could have chosen to surrender, but the end result would still have been the same. He'd been accused of murder, three eyewitnesses prepared to testify against him, and conviction meant an act of blood atonement for his soul's sake. Skousen hadn't cared to face a court and firing squad, preferred to try his luck with pistols, only to discover that he had none left.

It still surprised the rider that his quarry had not recognized him, walking into camp at sundown with the fire's light on his bearded face. He was a well-known figure in the territory, and particularly in the capital at Salt Lake City: three full inches over six feet tall, with dark hair pulled back from a high forehead and falling past his shoulder blades. It wasn't vanity that made him think the fugitive should know his face by sight, just common sense.

Few other members of the church and state that served it had achieved the fame—some said, the notoriety—of Orrin Porter Rockwell.

Still, there'd been no hint of recognition in the killer's eyes when he had welcomed Rockwell to his fireside. Skousen had given a false name— Jack Sloan—then froze as Rockwell spoke his own, drawing aside his coat's lapel to bare the U.S. marshal's badge he wore pinned to his buckskin shirt. The same move cleared one of his Colt Navy revolvers, situated for a cross-hand draw, its seven-inch barrel tucked under his gun belt.

Skousen's pistol wasn't showing, but he tried to reach it anyhow, cursing and fumbling underneath his jacket. Rockwell sat and watched him struggle, likely could have reached across the fire and clubbed him senseless with the Colt, but what would be the point? Dead here, or dead in Salt Lake City ten days hence. What difference did it make?

He'd waited until Skousen had the pistol in his hand—the Colt Dragoon he'd used to kill a shopkeeper in Bountiful—then drew and drilled his forehead with a shot at point-blank range. The Colt Navy's slug was relatively small, only .36 caliber to the Dragoon's .44, but more than large enough to do its job. Skousen was dead before his shoulders hit the cold, hard ground, and he had barely twitched thereafter.

Rockwell did feel sorry for the killer's roan mare, forced to haul his carcass back some eighty-odd miles through the Wasatch range and desert, over ground it had already covered heading eastward. Not the horse's fault. Its owner should have known that there was no escaping from the vengeance of the Lord, in this world or the next.

When he was close enough to smell the city, Rockwell let his thoughts range on ahead of him, plotting what he should do once he'd delivered Skousen's body to the chief of police. Rockwell had no family to deal with at the moment, having left his first wife and their three children in Missouri, twelve years earlier. Luana Beebe Rockwell had quickly found another husband and was sealed to him within a week of Rockwell's lighting out, which put his mind at ease and let him deal with business more pragmatically. He might decide to marry sometime in the future, yet again, but would not be encumbered with a gang of thirty-odd like Prophet Joseph Smith, much less the forty-nine who trailed around behind the governor.

What he required this evening was, first, a bath, and then a good hot meal, perchance at Burtis Cloward's restaurant. Beyond that, he looked forward to a night's sleep in his own bed, without smelling horses or the dead man he'd been hauling for the past five days.

Rockwell entered Salt Lake City from the eastern end of Temple Street, feeling the change from dirt to cobblestones under his horse's hooves. The street was wide and lined with tall, well-tended trees—no minor undertaking in the middle of a desert, where the nearest lake was saltier than any ocean on the globe.

The heart of town was Temple Square, picked out by Brigham Young himself upon arrival of the Saints, eleven years ago. A wall had been erected to surround it soon thereafter, the beginning of a tabernacle, followed shortly by construction of a Council House in 1852, for governance of Deseret—now Utah Territory—and in 1855 the city's first true public building, the Endowment House, used for administering temple rituals until the mammoth tabernacle was completed, sometime in the future. Its plot had not been dedicated until February 1853, with the corner stone laid two months later.

Some might have asked what took so long, but they'd be unfamiliar with the troubled history of Rockwell's faith. He had been a child of seven years, and ignorant, when Prophet Joseph Smith received his First Vision in 1820, only seventeen when he was baptized into the Church of Jesus Christ of Latter-day Saints at Canandaigua, New York. The Gentile persecution had begun that same year, 1830, driving the Saints first into Ohio, then to Jackson County, Missouri, where Rockwell had married Luana Beebe at the Big Blue settlement, in February 1832. By October of the next year, vigilante forces had expelled the Saints from the community they'd dubbed New Zion, with the bulk of them retreating to Kirtland, Ohio.

They'd built a temple there, with some degree of opulence, but schism in the ranks drove the majority to try Missouri once again, in 1837, hoping Gentile attitudes had changed. They hadn't, even though the Saints had tried their luck in Caldwell County that time, with a settlement they called Far West. Harassment had continued, and Rockwell had enlisted with the Danites—Prophet Smith's "avenging angels"—when their order was founded in June of 1838. A month later, he'd been ordained as an LDS deacon. Tension had turned to shooting during August, escalating through October, until Governor Lilburn Boggs had issued Executive Order No. 44, declaring that "the Mormons must be treated as enemies, and must be exterminated or driven from the State if necessary for the public peace." After the Haun's Mill Massacre, Major General Samuel Lucas of the state militia had laid siege to Far West, compelling the Saints to surrender on November 1.

Prophet Smith and sixty other leaders of the church had been convicted of treason that same day, General Lucas scheduling their mass execution for the next morning, but General Alexander Doniphan defied that order, threatening mutiny if it was carried out. Embarrassed, Lucas had surrendered his prisoners for trial in civil court, with the list of defendants shortened to Smith and four others. Convicted once again, the five had managed to escape on April 15, 1839, with the connivance of their guards, while being transferred from Clay County's jail to state prison. Investigators later claimed the sheriff and his deputies were drunk on duty, but the truth was that the break had been permitted to relieve Missouri's governor from federal reprisals for his now-notorious extermination order.

After their getaway, Smith and the others joined the Saints who'd fled Missouri in the nearby town of Commerce, Illinois. Rockwell was there to greet them, joining the celebration, and remaining when they bought the town in April 1840, changing its name to Nauvoo. Taken from Hebrew, in the fifty-second Chapter of Isaiah, that translated as "How beautiful upon the mountains." Four years after their arrival, there were some twelve thousand Saints in town, with Nauvoo rivaling Chicago on Lake Michigan, for size. Its residents were hopeful that their faith might find a more humane reception from its neighbors.

Wrong again.

As the LDS population increased, non-Mormons in the nearby towns of Carthage and Warsaw began agitating against them, convinced that the church was a threat to their power within Hancock County. They may have been right, in political terms, since the Saints voted more or less in lock-step—or they had, until the early part of 1844. That January, William Law had fallen out with Prophet Smith over the principle of plural marriage, drawing off some like-minded dissenters into a splinter sect they called the True Church of Jesus Christ of Latter Day Saints. Law's newspaper, the *Nauvoo Expositor*, published a single issue blasting Smith, before the city council voted it a public nuisance and empowered Smith to have the press destroyed. Rockwell had been among those who performed that duty, on June 10, and thereby struck a spark that had disastrous results.

Smith was arrested with his brother, Hyrum, and the other city council members on June 25, confined at Carthage pending trial on charges of riot and treason, but they never had their day in court. On June 27, two hundred Gentiles with blackened faces stormed the Carthage jail and shot both brothers in their cell, then tried to take the Prophet's head for bounty. Rockwell couldn't vouch for claims that lightning drove the lynchers off, since he had missed the whole event and still regretted failing to arrive and intervene.

Or die in the attempt.

What followed was another in the string of so-called "Mormon wars," this one in Illinois, where legislators had revoked the Nauvoo charter in January 1845. The town survived a while in spite of that, and Rockwell was ordained there, as a high priest of the church, on January 5, 1846. Ex-wife Luana was sealed to second husband Alpheus Cutler nine days later, with no hard feelings voiced on either side. By then, Rockwell was standing guard for Brigham Young, President of the Quorum of Twelve Apostles, and when the church moved west en masse, Rockwell had been a member of the Vanguard Company that broke the Mormon Trail.

A long and bitter thirteen hundred miles that

was, from Winter Quarters north of Omaha to Salt Lake Valley, then in territory claimed by Mexico. It took the better part of three months to deliver 444 Saints and three black servants, losing none along the way despite a rash of mountain fever borne by fat, blood-sucking ticks. The exodus from Nauvoo had begun in earnest then, bringing two thousand Saints to Salt Lake City by year's end.

The rest was history.

Police Chief Jeremiah Fordyce was a stocky man, mid-forties, with a sour attitude and face to match, as if the troubles he witnessed daily were too much for him to swallow and they'd started festering inside him. Coming out at sight of Rockwell through his office window, he was putting on his black hat, polishing his chief's badge with his fingers.

"Marshal Rockwell."

"Chief Fordyce."

"That be Heber Skousen underneath the tarpaulin?"

"The very same."

"No point in asking whether he surrendered."

"He did not."

"Hmm."

"I'll leave him in your hands, then, and await my just reward."

"Reward?"

"A hundred dollars, I recall, was offered by the victim's kinfolk."

"Hmm."

"You said that."

"What?"

"Shall I collect from you, or talk to them in Bountiful?"

"I'll see you get what's coming to you, Marshal," Fordyce said.

And why not? Rockwell thought. His pay was meager, and deputies couldn't collect rewards offered by the federal government, on grounds that they drew salaries for tracking fugitives. On the other hand, rewards posted by private parties—individuals, some business, or a town— were all fair game.

Rockwell was turning from the chief, leading his horse, when Fordyce called out to his back, or maybe to the Appaloosa's rump, "The governor sent word he wants to see you."

"Fine," Rockwell replied, not slowing down. "I'll get washed up, something to eat."

"I got the sense he didn't want to wait. His messenger said *urgent.* Said it twice, in fact."

Rockwell stopped then and faced Fordyce. "What's it about?" he asked.

"Man didn't say," Fordyce replied, with something like a half smile. "Just said *urgent.* Twice."

CHAPTER 2

Going to see the governor could turn out good or bad. The *urgent* bit suggested that whatever Brigham Young might have in mind for Rockwell, it would not be pleasant. Then again, when was he ever called, except when there was trouble in the wind?

It wouldn't be the Utes. They'd been accepting of the Saints to start with, in the first six years or so of Deseret, then started pushing back at fresh incursions on their hunting grounds and slaughtered a Pacific Railroad survey party back in 1853, sparking what most whites called the Walker War because the Ute Chief, Colorow Walkara, also sometimes went by "Wakara" or "Walker." The six-month struggle wasn't much, as wars went, some two dozen killed on either side, and it had ended with the chief and his survivors being baptized in the church, summer of 1854. Baptism likely didn't take, in Rockwell's view, since when Walkara died in 1855, his wives, children, and fifteen horses got the hatchet and were buried with him, so he wouldn't have to roam around the Happy Hunting Ground alone.

If there was urgent trouble, Rockwell thought, it likely stemmed from Washington, where high and mighty Gentiles had their noses out of joint, trying to lord it over Utah territory and the Saints. Things had been peaceful in the State of Deseret until the Compromise of 1850 had established Utah Territory in its place, the residents allowed to vote on slavery despite their living well above the northern boundary for slave states Congress had established twenty years before. Of course, the federals reserved the right to name leading officials in the territory, from the governor on down. President Fillmore got it right, appointing Brigham Young as governor, but the supreme court of the territory had two Gentile judges stacked against one Saint, and other offices were filled with carpetbaggers whose disdain for Mormon culture and the principle of plural marriage was notorious. By autumn 1851, three of the worst—two judges and Territorial Secretary Broughton Harris—had fled for home, claiming fear of assassination. They'd also stolen the territorial seal and $24,000 earmarked for public improvements, but Governor Young had declined Rockwell's offer to follow them and bring the money back, bloodstained or otherwise.

Matters had gone downhill from there, until James Buchanan took office as president in March 1857. He'd waited barely three months to mobilize troops under Colonel Edmund Alexander, marching to suppress a supposed rebellion in Utah Territory. Governor Young retaliated with a vow that Danite guerrillas would "bite the heels" of any federal troops who misbehaved within his jurisdiction, while Buchanan named a Gentile, Alfred Cumming, to replace Young as governor. Young considered secession, declared martial law, and revived the dormant Nauvoo Legion to repulse invaders. In the midst of all that, on September 15, longtime Mormon John Doyle Lee had led militiamen in slaughtering the Baker-Fancher wagon train at Mountain Meadows, killing some 120 emigrants in all. Reporting back to Young, Lee blamed Ute renegades for the attack, then spread the word that he had killed the travelers—"reluctantly," he claimed—on secret orders from the governor.

A lie that that Rockwell hoped to punish, soon as he was given leave to act.

The fumbling "Utah War" had stalled at that point, winter coming on, while the negotiators tried to work things out. Without an enemy to take the field against, Rockwell was left to do his duty as a U.S. marshal, tracking fugitives and bringing them to book, dead or alive.

Until now, when the governor demanded his attention.

Urgently.

The Council House was square, two stories tall, its sloping roof surmounted by a widow's walk of sorts, sprouting a cupola on top, complete with flagpole. A white picket fence, six feet tall, surrounded the property, its gate aligned with the building's entrance and guarded, these days, by members of the Nauvoo Legion.

Rockwell didn't know the young men on the gate that afternoon, but they apparently knew him. One of them nodded at him, called him "Brother," while the other opened up the gate, then closed it after him. Rockwell passed through the entryway, then turned left toward the staircase leading to the second floor and the governor's office.

Governor Young had a corner space upstairs, windows in two of his walls facing out over Main Street and South Temple. His office door was labeled with a brass plaque reading "PRESIDENT," a reference to his office in the church since Christmas 1847, though he'd also served as governor of Utah Territory for the past two years and some-odd days. Why advertise the lower rank, when it was known to everyone within five hundred miles already?

Rockwell knocked and waited, feeling suddenly self-conscious, as he always did before a meeting with the man thousands called an American Moses. There was no receptionist to meet him, just a booming call of "Enter!" from within, and Rockwell did as he was told.

Brigham Young was fifty-one years old, three or four inches shorter than Rockwell, but still an imposing figure. He was broad of chest and shoulder in his black frock coat and matching trousers, clean shaven, with dark hair parted on the left, long enough to cover his ears and his collar in back. Blue, almond-shaped eyes never left Rockwell's face as he closed the office door behind him, moving to stand before Young.

"Your quest was successful?" the governor asked him.

"It was, sir."

"Bad business. We cannot bear killers among us."

It wasn't a question, so Rockwell stood silent.

"Please sit, Brother Rockwell."

A chair was waiting for him, planted in front of the governor's large, hand-hewn desk. Rockwell waited for Young to assume his own seat, then sat. The desktop lay between them, polished to a glossy shine, with two neat stacks of paper separated by a foot or so of empty space where Young folded his hands.

"You are familiar with the settlement called Tartarus?"

"A mining town," said Rockwell. "On the east side of the Independence Range."

"Correct. And with the colony of Saints residing there?"

"Yes, sir." That group included Rockwell's nephew, Lehi, with some others and their wives. "They're digging silver."

"Which is vital to our territory, and of no small

value in our present difficulty with the Gentiles."

Once again, no response called for.

"Going back four months or so," the governor continued, "we have had reports of conflict in the Tartarus community, between our kinsmen and the local nonbelievers."

"Ah." The sound escaped, and then it was too late for Rockwell to retrieve it.

"Now," said Young, "we've lost communication altogether. I dispatched a man two weeks ago, to make a personal investigation and report his findings. It appears that he has fallen off the earth, as well."

Rockwell made hasty calculations in his head. Call it a hundred and ten miles one-way, to Tartarus, from Salt Lake City. A determined rider on a good horse could cover that distance in— what? Three days? Say a week for the round trip, with plenty of time left to spy out the landscape.

"Foul play?" Rockwell offered.

"I fear so." The governor half-turned to stare through a window at darkening sky. "I need to know what's happened, Brother Rockwell. You will go to Tartarus on my behalf. Discover the solution to this riddle."

"And?"

"And take whatever action you deem necessary, calling on your own experience and wisdom."

There it was.

"I'll leave first thing tomorrow, sir, unless—"

"That's fine," said Young. "Sleep well tonight. Our prayers go with you in the morning."

Rockwell rose to leave, thinking, *It won't be me who needs the prayers.*

CHAPTER 3

March 2, 1858

Rockwell was up an hour before the sun, which showed itself above the Uinta Mountains, east of Salt Lake City, at five minutes past the hour of 7:00 A.M. There was no trick to rising early if you set your mind to it, as any farmer could have told the lazy lay-abeds in town. Rockwell could ride with little or no sleep, and felt that he was downright pampered if he slept five hours in a given night.

By six, still dark, he had been dressed and fed, down at the livery to fetch his Appaloosa gelding, better rested than himself and feeling sassy, from the way it snorted when he put its saddle on. There'd be no pack horse for a simple three-day ride, when he could resupply in Tartarus before the homeward journey. He was carrying sufficient pemmican and corn dodgers to keep his stomach happy on the trail, plus oats to feed the gelding if they came up short of winter grass. Two canteens, just in case, though he expected to find water aplenty in the Stansbury Range, before he crossed the Great Salt Lake Desert. There'd be game, too, if he felt like hunting with the Sharps, but he was more inclined to hold off on the shooting if he could.

Rockwell wasn't concerned with meeting any federals along his route of travel. They'd gone into winter quarters, well east of the capital, for what the newspapers had called an "intermission" in their failed campaign to pacify the Saints. Meanwhile, an emissary out of Washington—one Thomas Leiper Kane of Philadelphia, a Gentile who had nonetheless befriended Mormons, leading a battalion of them in the war with Mexico—had sailed to Panama, then crossed the isthmus on a train and taken ship again to California, before he traveled overland to Salt Lake City for negotiations with the governor. They had been talking for a month, and Rockwell didn't know if they were getting anywhere, but skirmishing had ended when the first snows fell.

No, Rockwell thought. If he was ambushed on the way to Tartarus, it would be Indians. Shoshone, possibly. Maybe the Navajo, or Paiutes. Riding on his own, he'd look like easy pickings to a war party, and that would be their first mistake. Trying to take his hair would be the second, and the last that some of them, at least, would ever make.

Rockwell had nothing against Indians, per se. He understood their troubled history, as outlined on the golden plates that Prophet Smith had translated into the Book of Mormon. Red men were the sons of Laman, a son of the Hebrew prophet Lehi, who sailed to the New World with his brother Nephi, around 600 B.C. Some years after arriving, the two brothers had a bitter falling out, and Laman's followers—the Lamanites—drove their Nephite rivals into the wilderness, later eradicating them entirely. The risen Savior came to offer them his mercy, and while most accepted, after some two centuries they fell back into sin. Disgusted with them, God darkened their skin and cast them into spiritual darkness, leading heathen lives, estranged from Grace.

The Book of Mormon took its title from the name of a Nephite commander, whose son—Moroni, last survivor of the slaughtered tribe—inscribed that history on golden plates, delivered to the hands of Joseph Smith at Manchester, New York, in 1827. Smith, in turn, translated them and published the account in 1830, causing turmoil in the ranks of Gentiles who rejected the amendment to their own New Testament.

Damned fools.

As for the Lamanites of Utah Territory, call them by whatever names they happened to prefer, they had degenerated into savagery. That didn't mean they were immune to reason, necessarily, and some had willingly collaborated with the Saints when they arrived to form the State of Deseret, but farming on the shores of Great Salt Lake required expansion, white men pushing back the red until, at last, they met resistance.

Now, with everything from land and water to the native plants contested, it was often perilous for homesteaders and travelers outside of major towns.

It had become a matter of survival.

Rockwell was determined that the Saints would not be modern Nephites, hounded to extinction in the wilderness.

So, he would watch for red men on his way to Tartarus, but it was white men who concerned him more. Utah was not homogenous, in fact, although it had been settled by and for the Saints. Since their arrival, setting an example for success, Gentiles had slipped across the borders and established scattered settlements, mostly in search of gold, silver, or any other bounty from the earth that would enrich them overnight. They gave no thought to faith or family, only to tunneling for loot and wasting it in sin.

Of course, the governor was fond of gold and silver, too. The strike at Tartarus had seemed a boon from Heaven in its early days, but it had drawn the wrong sort eastward, men who'd tried their luck in California and gone bust, after the forty-niners beat them to the mother lode. From the high Sierras they had drifted, lusting for the next big strike, willing to do whatever might be necessary in pursuit of ore.

Willing to kill?

Of course.

The California gold rush had produced no end of bandits, claim-jumpers, and swindlers, followed in their turn by pimps and harlots, gamblers and saloon keepers. The same trash, doubtless, would be found in Tartarus—which stole its name from the very deepest pit of Hell.

Rockwell had not been there to see his nephew off, when Lehi left for Tartarus with his two wives. Another errand had demanded his attention, following a gang of brigands northward into Oregon Territory, running them to ground at a camp on the Fraser River. His federal badge had given Rockwell the authority he needed to pursue them, and to gun them down when surrender would have made them something less than men.

So they had died, and he had missed his nephew heading west.

Perhaps the last time that he could have seen Lehi alive.

He wasn't counting anybody out, just yet, but if the governor was worried, Rockwell took for granted that there had to be good reason. Brigham Young wasn't given to panic—nor Rockwell to mercy, where threats toward the Saints were concerned.

He hoped there was a simple explanation for the loss of contact with the Mormon colony at Tartarus. If not, he reckoned there'd be hell to pay.

Rockwell wasn't afraid of bloodshed, never had been. Some might say that was a flaw of character, but in his present line of work, he personally viewed it as a necessary trait. Some bad men didn't mind surrendering and spending time locked up, but most, in his experience, resisted the idea. More so, if they were looking at a noose instead of jail time. Why not try your chances in a fight, if it was death, regardless?

Most felons he had known would take a bullet over hanging, any day.

Another reason Rockwell didn't shy from killing was the blood atonement doctrine of his faith. The Book of Mormon was a little hazy on when felons ought to die, and how. In Chapter 24 of *Alma*, for example, God forgave the Lamanites for "many sins and murders," through the merits of his Son. After the death of Prophet Smith, however, Brigham Young had clarified the matter with an oath of vengeance, added to the Saints' endowment ritual.

In later sermons, Young elaborated on that theme. Boiled down to basics, there were certain sins that God would not forgive, without a spilling of the sinner's blood. Among the Saints, helping a lost soul toward its final exaltation was a gift of love. As Young asked from the pulpit, *Will you love that man or woman well enough to shed their blood?*

At times like this, thinking about his nephew's

family in Tartarus, Rockwell was filled to over-flowing with that love.

He made good time on his first day out of Salt Lake City, following the lake's shore for the most part, only passing through the northern foothills of the Stansbury Range, where fresh water was easy to find. He met no one along the way, a bonus, since he had no need of company when he was man-hunting. The night was cold, but Rockwell built a good fire, kept the Appaloosa close, his weapons near at hand.

Trail sleeping was a skill lawmen and soldiers learned from grim experience, knowing that if they fell too deeply into dreams, their waking might be brief—a blade across the throat, for instance—or they might not wake at all. When there were enemies about, and that was nearly always, dozing lightly ranked among the top survival skills.

Nothing disturbed his sleep that night, except coyotes howling at the moon, and he was on his own again the next day, as he crossed the desert. Jedediah Smith had lost a member of his party crossing that vast prehistoric lake bed, thirty years before, and it had slowed the Donner Party down enough, in 1846, that they were snowbound crossing the Sierras and reduced to eating human flesh. Rockwell did not intend to cross the worst part of the desert, though he'd done so in the past and lived to tell about it. This time, he was only angling off across its northern quadrant, on his way to Tartarus.

It struck him, even so, that the white wasteland spread before him made a fitting anteroom to Hell.

Millennia gone by, as Rockwell understood it, all that bone-bleached land had lain beneath Lake Bonneville, named for the Frenchman who was first to lay white eyes upon it, back in 1833. The Great Salt Lake and scattered others were the remnants of that inland sea, while most of it— some nineteen thousand square miles, overall— had been reduced to salt and sand.

Despite its blighted history, the desert still supported plant life—tumbleweeds and sego lilies, buckwheat, golden poppies, blue grama and wildflowers in season—with the kinds of animals you would expect in barren places: lizards, scorpions, sidewinders, roadrunners, and the coyotes that were prone to wail by night. None of them troubled Rockwell's sleep, once he had thrown a lariat around his blanket to deter cold-blooded visitors, waking to stoke the fire as necessary through the night.

The trick to getting by in solitude, Rockwell had learned, was living on the inside of his head and being comfortable with his memories. He'd never killed a man who, in his estimation, didn't have it coming. As for him abandoning Luana and the kids, he'd known she couldn't stay the course that lay before him, dealing with the Gentile persecutions, the avenging fallen Saints and hunting outlaws. She was settled now, and Rockwell felt no guilt for anything he'd done.

Sleep wasn't troublesome. He had a nightmare now and then, like anybody else, but woke without remembering its substance. There were no ghosts haunting him—or, if there were, he couldn't see them and they never spoke to him. He'd known Danites who lost their nerve for the gun work, claiming that the dead ones stood before them when they closed their eyes, but Rockwell saw that as a deficit in character. A loss of faith.

Not something he'd been troubled with, so far.

His second night of camping out was much the same, except that he burned tumbleweeds and greasewood through the night, instead of fir and pine. It did the job, but needed frequent tending to preserve a constant flame. Third morning of the trip, he had the Appaloosa loaded and was on his way before the first true light of dawn arrived to warm the desert flats.

And started thinking about Tartarus.

Rockwell had never seen the settlement, but from experience, he knew all mining towns were more or less the same. The ones he'd visited were short on decent women, long on sin, and focused on accumulating riches to the virtual exclusion of all else. Sometimes preachers tried their luck among the avaricious heathens, but they usually didn't last long, either moving on or being sucked into the general corruption that surrounded them.

It would be different, he hoped, with Lehi and the other Saints the governor had sent to mine for silver when the strike was made. Cast in with Gentiles, they were bound to face temptation, ridicule, perhaps abuse—unless they fell in with the pack, that is. Rockwell considered which was worse, corruption or a martyr's fate, and didn't have to think about it very long.

He'd go down fighting, rather than surrender to the call of Mammon, any day.

Maybe tomorrow, or the next day, if he found what he expected in the mining town.

He had his orders: *Take whatever action you deem necessary, calling on your own experience and wisdom.* Meaning deal with anyone who'd harmed a Saint as he saw fitting.

Blood atonement.

Rockwell knew what he had to do. Search out the law in Tartarus, if there was any to be found, and state his business. Show his badge to settle any argument over authority, and get directions to the Mormon camp. Find Lehi and the rest, if they were still there to be found. And if not, learn what had become of them. Lacking a lawman to interrogate, he'd press the question elsewhere.

Simple.

Except that towns with dirty secrets had a way

31

of holding onto them. Hunting a fugitive with money on his head was one thing. Anyone might give him up for part of the reward, or just the feeling that they'd done the decent thing. Guilt shared amongst the populace was something else, again. In that case, breaking silence was as good as a confession, bearing retribution home.

And Rockwell was the Reaper.

Probably, his reputation would precede him. That could either help or work against him, all depending on the stories that had found their way to Tartarus. Lawman or executioner? And was there any difference to speak of, in the end?

If he was feared, so much the better. Men might think twice about challenging him, maybe even lying to his face. But if they feared so much that they were dumbstruck . . . well, he'd have to find a way to loosen up their tongues.

Third afternoon, an hour past midday, his eyes picked out the blot of Tartarus on the northwest horizon, looming gradually larger as he closed the distance at a walking pace. The Appaloosa had done well, and Rockwell didn't want to punish it unnecessarily. He'd reach the settlement in due time, ample daylight still remaining for the first phase of his task.

He didn't know what to expect beyond trouble, so Rockwell had seen to his weapons that morning, before breaking camp. Both of his Navy Colts were fully loaded, and he carried two spare loaded cylinders to save time, if he used the first twelve rounds. He carried paper cartridges and bullets for his .52-caliber Sharps rifle in a bandolier of pouches, slung across his chest. The Bowie in his boot, for this trip, had been supplemented with a tomahawk, nineteen-inch handle, well balanced for throwing.

Whatever waited for him in the mining town, Rockwell felt he was ready.

And he would be meeting it head-on.

CHAPTER 4

Tartarus was more or less as Rockwell had imagined it. Saloons lined both sides of the town's main street, no doubt with cribs upstairs for working girls. Other amenities included two competing hardware stores with gear for prospectors, a hotel and a restaurant, a barbershop with bathtubs in the back, a blacksmith and a livery, an assay office, and a laundry operated by Celestials. Small houses ranged back from the main drag without any seeming plan, and Rockwell guessed that many of the local miners would be sleeping at their claims, in tents or shanties. When it rained, the street would be a sea of mud, but winter had it chilled rock-solid with a light dusting of snow.

He found the local law wedged in between two of the town's saloons, the Gold Dust and the Lucky Strike. A small sign on the door announced POLICE. Rockwell tethered his Appaloosa to the hitching rail in front of it and took his rifle with him when he went inside. Just playing safe.

The law in Tartarus was forty-some years old and heavy-set, running to fat, with salt-and-pepper hair under a rolled-brim hat. When Rockwell walked into his little office, he was dozing, kicked back in a chair, boots resting on a corner of his desk. He didn't hear the front door opening, so Rockwell pushed it shut with more force than the job required, causing the marshal—constable, whatever he might call himself—to jerk awake and drop his feet.

"Help you?" he asked, resentfully.

"I hope so."

Bleary eyes had focused now, and spotted Rockwell's badge. The marshal stood and came halfway around the desk, then stopped, not offering his hand. "Rance Fowler. I'm chief of police in Tartarus. And you are . . . ?"

"Porter Rockwell." Fowler had already seen his badge; no need to mention it.

"That rings a bell," said Fowler.

"Does it?"

"You're the one who tried to kill that gov'nor. Back in Illinois, was it?"

"Missouri. And it wasn't me."

Frowning. "They tried you for it, didn't they?"

"Tried and acquitted."

Lack of evidence, the way the verdict read, although he *had* been handed a five-minute sentence for attempted jailbreak, prior to trial.

"I heard somewhere you bragged about it."

"You heard wrong."

"What makes somebody do a thing like that, you think? Shoot at a gov'nor."

"First thing, he was out of office when it happened, better than a year. In May of 'Forty-

35

two, it was. And second thing, I never shot *at* anybody in my life. When I shoot somebody, he's shot and stays that way. Boggs is alive, ain't he?"

"He is that. Come west back in 'Forty-six, from what I hear. A big cheese out in Californy."

"Maybe I'll run into him sometime."

"You always wear your hair like that?"

"Like what?" Rockwell pretended that he didn't understand.

"I never seen a white man with his hair that long, is all."

December 1843, after the verdict handed down in Carthage, Rockwell had arrived in Nauvoo in the middle of a snowstorm, filthy and ragged, interrupting a Christmas party at the Prophet's home. Once the trail-worn scarecrow was identified, he had been favored with a special blessing, Joseph Smith himself pronouncing it. "I prophesy, in the name of the Lord," Smith had declared, "that so long as ye shall remain loyal and true to thy faith, you need fear no enemy. Cut not thy hair and no bullet or blade can harm thee."

And so it had been, from that day to this. As Rockwell's hair grew longer, so did the list of men he'd faced and vanquished in killing situations. Too bad the Prophet hadn't blessed himself, to keep from being murdered with his brother, six months later.

"I don't care for barbers much," said Rockwell.

Keep it simple. "Can we talk about our business?"

"What would that be?"

"I need to find some of your local residents."

"Got names?"

He had a list but didn't feel like reading it aloud for Fowler. "You'd be well aware of them," he said. "They're Saints."

"Saints, is it?" Fowler smiled, a hint of mockery behind it. "Ain't they all in Heaven?"

Rockwell kept his face deadpan. "Mormons," he said. "How's that?"

Fowler's good humor did a fade. "We had some Mormons hereabouts," he granted. "Eight or nine of 'em, I'd estimate. They pulled up stakes about a month ago. I guess their claim played out. Maybe the weather didn't suit 'em."

"Pulled up stakes."

"The way I heard it."

"Going where?"

The chief's shrug made his belly wobble underneath his wrinkled shirt. "The hell if I know. People come and go, a town like this. They don't check in or out with me."

"That claim you mentioned. Where would that be found?"

"You plan on goin' out there, Marshal?"

"Might do."

"Well, now, someone else is workin' it, these days."

"Working a played-out claim?"

Another shrug. "Nobody said prospectors are the smartest folks around. They see someone's been scratchin' at the dirt and left, some figure all the hard work's done."

"Would they be right?"

The chief was frowning now. "Not sure I follow you."

"You've heard of claim-jumping, I guess."

"Oh, sure. It happens, true enough. Outside my jurisdiction, but we got a miner's court to deal with things like that. They take a hard line, too."

"You'd definitely know about it if a family was run off, then." Pinning him down.

The chief seemed hesitant to answer, but he squeezed it out. "I reckon so."

"All right, then. You just show me to the claim in question, and—"

"Can't help you, there. Matter of jurisdiction, like I said."

"You can't set foot outside of town? Is that the story?"

"Well . . ."

"Because, I never heard of any law like that."

"No, no. I just got lotsa work to do, right now." Fowler waved one hand vaguely toward the papers littering his desk.

"Like you were working when I came in here?"

"Long nights'll wear you down. A man of your experience knows that."

"Directions, then."

"Well, sure. You head north out of town, then—"

"Write it out for me."

The chief turned toward his desk, handbills, letters and WANTED posters spread across its surface without any semblance of organization. "It looks like I got lotsa paper," he said, "but this stuff's all official. I can't just—"

As he spoke, Rockwell crossed the small office and took Heber Skousen's poster down from the bulletin board. "You can use this."

"That's—"

"Cancelled."

"Who cancelled it?"

"*I* cancelled *him,*" Rockwell said.

"Ah. All right then."

Fowler rummaged in a desk drawer till he found a pencil, then drew a crude map on the back of the poster, including an arrow marked "N" for direction. An "X" marked the end of a straggling trail, north by northwest from town.

"That's the spot where your saints used to dig. Call it two miles and change. But they're gone, like I said."

"Yeah, I heard you."

"Don't know if you've been around miners too much. Some are touchy, you go snooping into their business."

"Their business means nothing to me," Rockwell said. Not adding the thought, *If it* is *their business.*

"Okay, then. You'll have no trouble."

"People always say that."

"And?"

"They're right, 'bout half the time."

He left the chief to mull that over, fetched his horse, and walked it to the misnamed Grand Hotel. Tied up again, another hitching rail, and entered through a sparsely furnished lobby with bare floorboards and a smelly coat of fresh paint on the wall. Some pink color Rockwell had never seen in nature. It set off the mottled cheeks of the reception clerk, a youngster in his twenties with a head of curly hair already creeping back around the temples. Ten years on, he'd likely have the coiffure of a billiard ball.

"Yes, sir!" he greeted Rockwell. "Welcome to the Grand Hotel!"

"You got a room to spare?"

"Of course, Mister . . . um, Marshal. Are you traveling alone?"

Rockwell took time to peer around the lobby. "Seems so."

"Right, then! Rooms are three dollars a night."

"Expensive."

"Well . . ."

"No matter." He'd get reimbursement from the Marshals Service, or the governor.

"Then, if you'd kindly sign the register . . ."

The book sat on a kind of swivel, which the clerk half-turned to face it Rockwell's way. He took a dip pen from its inkwell on the counter, handing it to Rockwell, who inscribed his name on the first empty line.

"And may I ask how long you might be staying with us, Marshal Rockwell?"

"You can ask, but I don't know. Depends how my investigation goes."

"Investigation? My, that sounds intriguing."

"Does it?"

"Well . . . I mean . . . a mystery?"

"Of sorts."

"Well, sir, I hope you solve it."

"I intend to."

"Here's your key, then, Marshal. Room nine on the second floor, facing the street. If you need help with any luggage—"

"No." Then Rockwell had a thought. "About that mystery."

"Yes, sir?" The clerk leaned forward, eyes asparkle.

"What I'm looking into is a group of Mormons." Careful not to call them Saints, this time. "Police chief tells me that they worked a claim out north of town, then up and left."

The clerk, his eyes no longer bright, eased back and swallowed something that prevented him from answering right off. "Mormons? We don't have any staying with us at the moment."

"Well, there's one."

"There is? Oh." Catching it. "I see. Yes, sir."

"I didn't ask you whether they were *here*."

"I don't know much of anything about the mining claims, Marshal. Now, if you talked to the police chief—"

"Done and done. He's given me directions to their claim. Their *former* claim, that is. X marks the spot."

"Well, then."

"My job is finding out what happened to them."

"Happened?" Wheezing just a little.

"Where they went," Rockwell amended. "See if I can track them down."

"Afraid I couldn't help you there, sir."

"No? Well if you stumble over somebody who could, feel free to tell them where I'm staying, will you? I'd be pleased to meet them."

"Yes, sir. Absolutely. But it's not the kind of thing I'm likely to uncover."

"Who knows, eh? We live and learn."

He took his saddlebags up to the room and found it clean enough, if Spartan. Furnishings, besides the bed, included a sideboard and mirror, one plain wooden chair, a basin, pitcher, and a chamber pot. Filling the pitcher or dumping the pot meant a hike to the fenced yard in back, where a pump stood close beside the back door, and a privy occupied the farthest southeast corner.

It was still mid-afternoon, but Rockwell didn't feel like riding out, just then, to see the claim his people had supposedly abandoned without sending word to Salt Lake City. He preferred to make that ride tomorrow, once he'd had an early breakfast. Maybe catch the new claim holders shaking off their night chills, still a little groggy, and amenable to putting off their work a bit while Rockwell asked some questions.

But amenable or not, he'd hear their answers.

In the meantime, he'd have supper, drift around the town some, asking questions where he thought they'd have the most impact. Like dropping pebbles in a pond and watching ripples spread. Talk to the merchants he deemed likely to remember gossip. Later, he supposed some of the miners would be coming in to drink, gamble, and patronize the nanny shops. Rockwell could talk to them, as well, and find out what they knew.

If none admitted knowing anything, that ranked as information, in itself.

Before feeding himself, he had the Appaloosa to take care of. Rockwell left his rifle and his tomahawk inside in his hotel room, made certain that the door was locked, then walked his horse down to the livery. The hostler was a grizzled character who wore the disappointments of a long life on his face, but he was obviously fond of animals. Rockwell made the arrangements, paid for one night in advance, then wandered out to take a closer look at Tartarus.

It had been well and truly named, he thought.

The town—not a *community,* he couldn't call it that by any stretch of the imagination—was a monument to Mammon. If it had a guiding principle, it would be lust: for silver, for the warm oblivion of alcohol, for pleasures of the flesh. Rockwell had trouble picturing his nephew and the other Saints in Tartarus, buying supplies or visiting the assay office. Everything they saw must have repelled them.

Or, were they seduced by the enticements of this little Hell on Earth?

Rockwell dismissed that thought immediately. If the colony had simply sold their faith for silver, why would the police chief say they'd pulled up stakes and left? To seek their fortune elsewhere in the world, without the simple courtesy of a farewell to loved ones left behind?

Unthinkable.

From apprehension, Rockwell's mind had shifted toward conviction that there must have been foul play involved. His job: to find the individuals responsible and mete out fitting punishment.

The only restaurant in town was called Delmonico's. The waitress tried to seat him at a table by the broad front window, but he chose a corner place instead, where he could watch the room and have his back against a solid wall. Precautions mattered in a strange place—and familiar ones, sometimes.

The other diners were not too dissimilar from Rockwell. Most were rugged-looking men, although he counted three with women at their tables. Wives, perhaps, and modestly attired, but sporting painted lips and cheeks colored with rouge. Rockwell attracted some attention—for his hair, his height, his brace of pistols—though he would have said the other men were more or less unkempt, and nearly all of them were armed.

He ordered beefsteak, beans and fried potatoes on the side, with black coffee to wash it down. Saints were discouraged from imbibing stimulants—"hot drinks," according to the Word of Wisdom handed down by Prophet Smith—but Rockwell made exceptions for a situation such as this, where he was trail-weary and had to stay alert. Meat eating was also restricted to winter or times of famine, and the rare steak he received made Rockwell thankful for the cold outside.

He took his time at supper, studying the other patrons of Delmonico's, eavesdropping on the chat from nearby tables when he could. As he expected, nothing that he overheard was helpful to his mission, but he got a better feeling for the people. Mostly, they discussed the price of silver and the probability of striking paydirt. Some had tried their luck before, in California, but had either failed to strike it rich, or—so they claimed, laughing at their own foolishness—

spent everything they earned on liquor, women, or at gaming tables.

Rockwell couldn't overhear the female diners, seated at a greater distance from his corner table, but they seemed intent on smiling, sometimes laughing, at whatever their companions had to say. He calculated that they knew which side their bread was buttered on, and aimed to please.

The waitress came around when he was finished, and he let her talk him into apple pie. The slice she brought was large and fresh, served with a smile that Rockwell might have found inviting under other circumstances. As it was, while not suspecting her specifically of any ill intent, Rockwell had made his mind up not to trust a living soul in Tartarus unless they gave him ample cause.

So far, none had.

While he was busy with his meal, and then dessert, various diners left Delmonico's and were replaced by others of the same sort: rough men, for the most part, who had tried to make themselves presentable, but who would still have raised eyebrows if they'd intruded on polite society. Aside from grimy fingernails, unruly hair, and weapons, they were drawn and haggard, many of them anxious looking, as if they expected someone to come by and snatch the food off of their plates.

A consequence of guarding claims, Rockwell

surmised—or, maybe, guilty consciences. Prospectors were a rowdy lot, in his experience, with checkered pasts. Some of them might be wanted men, but Rockwell didn't recognize their faces from his stock of posters back in Salt Lake City. Any fugitives among them were secure, for now, while he attended to the business of the missing Saints.

When he could stall no longer, Rockwell left a dollar on his table, rose, and made a point of not acknowledging the eyes that followed him as he proceeded toward the exit. If he struck them as a bit mysterious, prompted some gossip on his own account and got the townsfolk asking questions, it might work to his advantage. He supposed Chief Fowler must have talked to someone since their interview, and possibly the hotel clerk had passed his name around, as well.

All to the good.

The value of a reputation was the impact that it had on strangers. And if it had been exaggerated somewhat in the telling, why, so much the better. Even the hardest man might hesitate to call out a notorious bloodletter.

Take the thing with Lilburn Boggs, for instance, in Missouri. Was it Rockwell's fault the former governor survived, despite two buckshot pellets in his head and two more in his neck? A team of doctors had pronounced him close to death, and one newspaper even published his obituary.

Miracles *did* happen, seemingly, and Boggs was spared to meet his fate another time. In custody, Rockwell professed that he'd "done nothing criminal," and evidence was lacking at his trial, despite claims from a turncoat Saint—the loathsome traitor John Cook Bennett—claiming Prophet Smith had personally touted Rockwell as the triggerman.

All ancient history.

Tonight, he had new work cut out for him.

He was embarking on a walking tour of Hell.

CHAPTER 5

"I'm tellin' you," Rance Fowler said, "he knows that somethin's up."

"He can't *know* anything, unless you let it slip," Paul Beardsley answered back.

"I never did!" Fowler protested.

"Then you're sweating over nothing," Isaac Walton said.

"Nothin'." The echo came from Emil Jacobs.

They were seated at a table in a back room of the Lucky Strike, one of the three saloons that Beardsley owned in Tartarus, together with the restaurant and one of the two hardware stores. In fact, he was the mayor as well, a post secured by doling out free whiskey on Election Day. From that position, he'd installed Walton as Justice of the Peace, and Fowler as the town's chief of police. The only semi-independent operator in the room was Jacobs, chairman of the local Miner's League. A bottle sat in front of them, filled glasses all around.

"Nothin' to sweat about?" Fowler could feel his agitation mounting by the second. "Did you hear me tell you he's a U.S. marshal?"

"So?" Beardsley was unimpressed.

"He's Porter Rockwell. Jesus, Paul, he's killed more men than strychnine."

"That's a lotta talk the church puts out," Jacobs opined. "He's just a man, like anybody else."

"You think so?" Fowler's tone was dubious.

"Rance, you're the law in Tartarus," Walton reminded him. "What you say goes."

"I don't outrank no U.S. marshal. He's got jurisdiction over all the territory. Hell, the *country.*"

"Doesn't matter," Beardsley said. "He's askin' questions, Chief. That's all. If nobody splits fair with him, there's nothin' he can do. It's *your* job to make sure the lid stays on."

"You wanna tell me how? I can't go up and down the street, here, tellin' people not to talk to him."

"No need for that," said Jacobs. "Ever'body in the know is smart enough to keep their mouth shut, anyhow."

"You *hope* so," Fowler said.

"Well, if they ain't, then find a way to shut 'em up."

"Hold on, now." Fowler didn't care for the direction this was heading.

"Hold on, nothin'," Jacobs said. "You're in this thing as deep and dirty as the rest of us. It's too damn late to start pretendin' that your hands are clean."

"Now, Emil—"

"What he's sayin'," Beardsley interrupted, "is that we're all partners here. We saw an opportunity and took it. Some of us may feel we only did a little, but the law don't see it that way. If this goes before a court outside of Tartarus, we swing together. Ever'body's clear on that, I hope."

"Judge in Salt Lake can only hang us once," said Jacobs. "An' I do mean *all* of us."

"Listen, now," Fowler replied. "It ain't just those who lent a hand we have to think about. Nine people don't just up and disappear without somebody noticin'. You think nobody's let a word slip since? When they was drunk, up in the cribs, wherever?"

"Doesn't matter," Beardsley said again. "This was a matter planned and carried out *in common,* for the benefit of Tartarus."

Your benefit, more like it, Fowler thought, but kept it to himself as Paul went on.

"Now, on reflecting, some might say we made the *wrong* decision, but it's done. Can't be *un*done. And those who share the benefits of what was done—the *sacrifice* we made for Tartarus—have got no call to judge whoever took the lead."

"It ain't their judgment that concerns me," Fowler said. "Rockwell—"

"There you go again," Jacobs cut in. "He's just a man."

"A man who's got the law behind him, *and* the church," Fowler replied.

"You got religion now?" asked Jacobs.

"It ain't about religion."

"Well, what *is* it, then?"

"I'm tellin' you, it's *Porter Rockwell.*"

Beardsley frowned, shaking his head. "You're lettin' gossip build him up into a bogeyman. He gets too close, I guarantee he bleeds like anybody else."

"Oh, wonderful. You think the government won't send more marshals? Or that Brigham Young won't send his Danites?"

"I heard Rockwell *was* a Danite," Walton said.

"Worse yet," said Fowler.

"What'n hell are Danites?" Jacobs queried no one in particular.

Fowler gaped at him. "You never heard of—"

"Skip that," Beardsley interjected. "If we have to bed him down, there's ways to do it so it don't come back on us."

"Like what?" asked Fowler.

"Do you want a list?" Beardsley replied.

Fowler considered it, then shook his head.

"Maybe it's better if you don't know, Chief," the mayor said. "Since you'd be the one called to investigate, and all."

Fowler drained off his whiskey glass, the liquor burning from his gullet down to his uneasy gut. "Guess I'll go on about my rounds, then, if we're done here."

"Good idea," said Beardsley. "On your way

out, see if Seamus Hannigan's still playin' faro, will you?"

"Sure." Another twinge of dark misgiving. "Do you wanna see him?"

"If he feels like he can tear himself away."

"Okay, then."

Fowler left them to it, closed the door behind him, and proceeded to the main barroom. Piano music welcomed him, off-key as usual, and loud enough to challenge normal conversation. Beardsley had a gold mine in the Lucky Strike, and didn't mind competing with himself for business with the Nugget and the Mother Lode. With half of the saloons in Tartarus under his thumb, you'd think he would be satisfied, but some men couldn't get enough.

Which brought them to their present pass.

Fowler found Seamus Hannigan, in fact, still playing faro. Losing, by the look of it, growing agitated as his money gravitated from his side of the table to the banker's. Fowler waited while the pimp lost yet another bet, then tapped him on the shoulder.

"What'n hell—?" Hannigan backed off from his snarl at sight of Fowler's badge. "Hey, Chief. You buyin' in?"

"You're cashin' out," Fowler replied.

The snarl came back. "That so?"

"Or, I can go tell Mr. Beardsley you don't wanna talk to him."

Hannigan blinked his one good eye, the other hooded by a scar across its lid. "He wants to see me?"

"If you got the time."

"Well, sure."

"Then go on back."

His duty done, Fowler proceeded through the drunken crowd and out into the dusky street.

Rockwell moved along the raucous central street of Tartarus, part of his mind amused at how well he seemed to fit in. He wasn't drunk, of course, and didn't reek of some harlot's cheap scent, but he could have been a prospector or trapper from the mountains, by the look of him. He was taller by four or five inches than most of the men who passed by him, broader of shoulder and chest, but his face had the same weathered quality found in the others.

Except for the gamblers, of course. By and large, they were soft men, and paler than most, since they commonly slept through the day and spent nights huddled over card tables. Gambling was banned by law in Utah Territory, but the news had clearly never made its way to Tartarus. The marshal, Fowler, obviously turned a blind eye to it—maybe even liked a game of chance himself, or took a portion of the proceeds to ensure that things ran smoothly.

None of that was Rockwell's problem, though

he speculated that he could have shut down the casinos in one night, if tasked to do so. All it took was the determination, possibly a show of force to start with. The elimination of resistance.

Not his job.

He drew curious glances from the patrons as he prowled through one saloon after another, only natural. As far as questions were concerned, he didn't talk to any of the bartenders. They might be fonts of information generally, but he calculated that they wouldn't talk unless he bought a drink, which wasn't happening. Another problem: none of them would know the missing Saints firsthand, since Mormons wouldn't rank among their customers.

What Rockwell needed was a miner—more than one, if possible—who knew the area and what went on outside of Tartarus. Someone to tell him who had come and gone, the past few months, and what had driven them to leave. If there'd been murder here, amongst the mines, the prospectors were bound to know.

But would they talk?

Perhaps, in certain circumstances. Liquor helped to loosen tongues and make a drinker careless, maybe sharing information he'd received in confidence or learned by chance. The other motive for unburdening a soul came down to personal emotions—guilt, fear, anger, jealousy, whatever. Even working with a drunkard, prying secrets loose took time and effort.

Getting started was the hard part. Prying into secrets called for a degree of privacy, so Rockwell couldn't join a poker game and casually ask the other players if they'd heard of any Mormons disappearing from the neighborhood. He needed to approach and cultivate informants individually, but again, there was a barroom protocol to be observed. A man you spotted drinking by himself was likely alone for a reason. Approaching his table without an invite—much less sitting down—could be awkward, and then some. Rockwell didn't look like a Mary, but mountain men were known for strange proclivities, and the last thing he needed was a brawl with some drunken miner who took his approach the wrong way.

His badge should cover that, but it could also silence people who possessed the information he required. Chief Fowler, he assumed, had spread the word of his arrival to the folks in Tartarus who mattered: his employers, any bigwigs with a major share of action in the town. Whether the news had filtered down to people on the street, or out among the mining claims, remained to be discovered. Rockwell thought of taking off his star, holding it back to show if someone took offense to nosy questions, then decided he was better off without concealing it and left it on his shirt, under the coat he wore against the March night's chill.

Over the course of three long hours, Rockwell spoke to half a dozen men in four saloons. He chatted with a couple of the painted ladies, too, then disappointed them when he declined a trip upstairs to see their cribs. At one place, called The Water Hole, a bouncer came around to ask his business and find out why Rockwell hadn't bought a drink. The badge persuaded him to move along, and also spoiled the mood he had been working on, his target vanishing into the night on thin, unsteady legs.

Long story short, the answers he received were variations on a theme of total ignorance. Trying to read expressions while the several men and women told him they knew nothing was a challenge, in itself. Some drinkers were the animated type, given to mugging and expansive gestures; others turned stone-faced when they were in their cups, and wouldn't flinch if they were set afire. Rockwell suspected that a couple of the men he'd spoken to were hiding *something,* but he couldn't pin it down.

Some folks looked guilty by default, when talking to the law.

A long, frustrating evening, but Rockwell didn't count it as a total waste. His face was known in town, now. He could be located and approached, if anyone was so inclined. Meanwhile, he'd get some sleep and, in the morning, pay a visit to the mining claim his fellow Saints had left to others when they disappeared into thin air.

Rockwell almost made it back to his hotel. He had less than a block to go, was looking forward to a bed instead of sleeping on the cold ground, when a woman stepped out of a recessed doorway just in front of him.

"Hey, there," she hailed him.

"Help you, ma'am?"

"It's possible." She looked him over in the dim light from the street. "You're new in town," she said, not asking.

"Does it show?"

"I would have noticed you before."

A stab at flattery. She could have said the same about a hunchback.

"As it happens, you're correct," he said.

"Out for some fun tonight?"

"Sorry. Fun's over. I'm just heading back to the hotel."

"You've got a *room*. That's better, yet."

"Ma'am—"

"Now, tell me somethin'. Do I look like *ma'am* to you?"

"I reckon not."

"You reckon right, Mister . . . ?"

"Rockwell."

"I'll bet you do."

That flustered him a little, not enough to matter. She was pretty, in a well-used kind of way, and he was only human, after all. And he was working, focused on his task to the exclusion of all else.

"I'll just be going now," he said.

"I don't think so." A male voice, coming from the alleyway behind him, to his left.

Rockwell half-turned in that direction, as a man six inches shorter than he emerged. The new arrival's face was shadowed, but it seemed to Rockwell that his left eye had been permanently closed somehow.

"Talking to me, friend?" he inquired.

"I is," the stranger answered. "And I ain't you's friend."

"Too bad. I could've introduced you to the lady."

"That's no *lady*," One-eye sneered at Rockwell. "That's my *woman* you been messin' with."

So that was it. Rockwell had heard about this dodge, of course, but never seen it acted out. A pimp set out one of his girls, then barged in to intimidate and rob a would-be customer. Which saved the girl from taking down her bloomers, anyway, but it was tougher on the mark and sometimes led to killing.

"There's been no messing, and you're welcome to her," Rockwell answered.

"Well, I never!" said the woman.

"Hard to swallow," Rockwell told her, paying more attention to the pimp.

"I ain't here for apologies," said One-eye.

"And I don't recall giving you one," Rockwell replied.

"Smart fella, eh?"

"Smarter than some I've met."

"Come into town and grab whatever takes your fancy, is it?"

"Haven't seen a thing that's caught it yet," said Rockwell. "If I do, I'll let you know."

The woman made a clucking sound of irritation, but remained well out of reach. No danger there, unless she had a pocket pistol hidden somewhere on her person. One-eye was the threat, no gun in sight, but he wore an Arkansas toothpick sheathed on his belt, right hand resting on its pommel.

"Now you's been disparagin'," the pimp replied, surprising Rockwell with his erudition. "You needs a lesson in deportment."

"Who's the teacher?" Rockwell asked.

"You're lookin' at him." As he spoke, the pimp flourished his blade, no less than fourteen inches long. Weighted for throwing, if the look of it was anything to go by.

Knife fighting was a last resort for Rockwell, saved for when a quiet killing was essential or he had run out of ammunition. As it was, he didn't feel the need to risk a slicing when he still had work to do in Tartarus.

"Guess there's no getting on your good side," he told One-eye, as he drew one of his Colts and cocked it.

"Hey, now!" One-eye said, too late.

The bullet drilled his right knee, cut the leg from under him, and dropped him to the wooden sidewalk. One-eye and the woman squealed in unison, one note nearly as high-pitched as the other. Rockwell kept his sobbing adversary covered as he stooped, retrieved the fallen dagger, then stepped back a pace.

"You made two big mistakes tonight," he told the pair of them. "First one was running your game on a lawman. Second was coming short-handed." To the fallen pimp, he said, "You won't be walking for a while. I'll probably be gone before you're on your feet again, but if you want to try and find me, come to Salt Lake City. Ask around for Porter Rockwell, when you're up to it. We'll finish what we started."

Turning toward the woman, Colt in one hand, toothpick in the other, Rockwell raised his pistol's muzzle to his hat brim. "Evening, ma'am," he said. "If there's a doctor in this burg, I'd recommend you run and fetch him for your friend. You want to talk to the police about this, chief knows where to find me."

"Bastard!"

"Just when I was thinking butter wouldn't melt," he said, and brushed on past her, leaving her to shift the crippled pimp if she was so inclined.

Or leave him lying where he was, for all that Rockwell cared. He didn't think there'd be a problem with Rance Fowler. He had read the chief as one who went along to get along. Fowler carried the law but closed his eyes to criminal infractions, so he'd have a hard time bracing Rockwell for an act of self-defense. If anything came of it, he would give Fowler his adversary's knife and file a charge of armed assault, maybe attempted murder. Let them deal with that while he went on about his business.

There was no clerk at the hotel's registration desk as Rockwell entered from the street, his Colt back underneath his belt, the confiscated dagger still in hand. He would have startled any guests, if they had met him in the lobby or ascending to the second floor, but Rockwell seemed to be the only creature stirring in the Grand Hotel.

He hoped it stayed that way, while he reloaded his revolver, used the privy, and got into bed. A good night's sleep would see him on his way to nephew Lehi's former claim, northwest of town.

And he would get some answers there, or know the reason why.

CHAPTER 6

Breakfast at Delmonico's was two fried eggs, a slab of ham, and biscuits drowned in gravy. Rockwell had a good start on it, chasing it with hot black coffee, when he saw Rance Fowler enter, peer around, then make his slow way back toward Rockwell's corner table. Rockwell concentrated on his food, but gave the chief a nod in the direction of his table's second chair.

"I understand you had a spot of trouble overnight," said Fowler, as he settled in.

"Trouble?"

"Seamus Hannigan."

"Don't know the man."

"You shot him?" Making it a question, like he wasn't sure.

"Oh, him. No trouble there."

"You wanna let me hear your side of it?"

Rockwell swallowed a slice of ham, then said, "Pimp and his nanny tried to pull a badger game on me. I didn't bite. He pulled a knife and ran against a pill. Simple."

"A knife, you say?"

Rockwell produced the toothpick from beneath his coat and dropped it on the table close to Fowler's folded hands. "Feel free to give it back, in case he wants to try his luck again."

"I'd guess he has another one by now," the chief replied.

"So, we're all done then." Working on the gravy biscuits.

"There was talk of Seamus filing charges."

"Should be interesting, once I've charged him with attempted murder of a U.S. marshal."

"Ain't the way him and the lady tell it."

"Lady." Rockwell tried to keep from smirking, but it wasn't easy.

"Claim the two o'them were strolling—"

"She was on the stroll, all right."

"—when you come up and make a rude remark to Annie."

"That her name?"

"It's what she calls herself."

"Which cathouse does she work in, Chief?"

"Well, now . . ."

"You want to charge me with assaulting Seamus and his Annie, go ahead. And good luck making the arrest."

Fowler began to fidget then, and lost some of the color from his face. He still had sand enough to say, "I don't appreciate a threat like that."

"I've never threatened anybody in my life," Rockwell replied. "Not you, nor old Missouri Boggs."

Another hesitation. Then, "Awright, if you say it was self-defense, that settles it as far as I'm concerned. The truth be told, that Seamus has a reputation that'd gag a buzzard."

Rockwell sipped his coffee. Waited. "So, we're done, then?"

"One more thing. You mind me askin' what your plans are for today?"

"Thought I might use that map of yours. Go out and see the claim you say the Saints abandoned. Meet the folks who took it over."

"You'll recall I mentioned—"

"Some of them are jumpy. Got it."

"I would hate for anything to happen there."

"Outside your jurisdiction, either way," Rockwell reminded him.

"That's true enough. I've done my part."

"Like Pilate."

"How's that?"

"Never mind."

"Mmm. You enjoy your breakfast, now."

"I'm trying to."

He watched the chief depart, making a left turn when he hit the sidewalk. Going where? Most likely to consult with someone higher up in Tartarus. Fowler didn't impress him as the sort who'd hatch a plot with pimps and prostitutes, if only for the reason that he lacked the nerve to follow through. So someone else had planned the badger game, or simply given Seamus Hannigan a free hand to proceed as he saw fit.

But it had backfired. They would have to think of something else.

When he was finished with his meal, Rockwell walked back to the hotel and used its privy, then retrieved his other tools—the Sharps and tomahawk. Fowler had left the toothpick lying on his breakfast table, where it gave the little waitress a surprise. Now Rockwell put it in his saddlebag and left it in his room, locked up, went back downstairs and out into the street.

Same hostler working at the livery. He knew Rockwell by sight, and went to get the Appaloosa, trailing small talk in his wake. "You leavin' us today, Marshal?"

"Can't say. I've got some things to see about. Save me a place."

"No prob'em."

For an old man, he was pretty spry. Rockwell stood watching while he got the Appaloosa saddled up within ten minutes, ready for the road. Rockwell doled out another coin to hold a stall, and got a grin back that was missing several teeth. If he was poison to the town, somehow, word evidently hadn't reached the hostler yet.

As for the people passing up and down Main Street, it may have been his own imagination that they eyed him with suspicion, apprehension, animosity. He saw none of the handful whom he'd questioned in his ramblings, after supper, but he guessed Chief Fowler would have spread the word to some extent by now. How far it spread, he reckoned, would depend on *who* knew *what* about the disappearance of his nephew and the other missing Saints.

The atmosphere surrounding Rockwell lightened once he'd cleared the northern boundary of Tartarus and put those anxious eyes behind him. He enjoyed riding the Appaloosa, but he wasn't on a pleasure jaunt. As soon as he was out of sight from town, Rockwell removed his Sharps from its saddle scabbard, resting it across his thighs and balanced by the saddle horn, ready for action. He was crossing open country, for the most part, on his ride to the abandoned Mormon claim, but any shooter with a weapon such as his might try to pot him from five hundred yards or more, and Rockwell wanted a response in kind at hand, if that occurred.

Meanwhile, he did his best to sit back and appreciate the scenery without imagining it as a battlefield. Not easy, given Rockwell's temperament and history. He'd tracked too many men, survived too many shooting scrapes, for any ride on hostile ground to feel like just another easy jaunt. And this *was* hostile ground, he sensed, no matter what Chief Fowler said about the Saints deciding on their own to pull up stakes and vanish in the wind.

An hour out of Tartarus, the land began to rise, taking him up into the foothills of the Independence range. Rockwell made no special study of geography, but knew the land of Utah Territory well enough for hunting game and men across its varied landscape. He knew, for instance, that the Independence Mountains ran north-south for roughly 110 miles, with their highest point—McAfee Peak—topping 10,400 feet. The mountaintops were white now, what the Spaniards called *Nevada*, meaning "snow-capped." Rockwell didn't plan on scaling them.

His business waited for him at the bleak foot of the range, where prospectors were bent on scratching treasure from the earth. Or stealing it from those who did the dirty work, if that was easier, and maybe getting rid of any pesky witnesses.

He didn't like to think of Lehi and the others being dead, but Rockwell was a realist—most would have said a pessimist or cynic. In a pinch, he wouldn't argue with them, wouldn't try to justify or balance his perspective with the basic optimism of his faith. Religion tried to see the good in human beings and redeem those who had gone astray. In Rockwell's line of trade, it made more sense to recognize an evildoer and proceed with any steps required to shut him down. The quickest way to wind up dead was scanning the world through rose-colored glasses.

How much farther? It was hard to tell, from Fowler's hand-drawn map, but from the chief's description of the distance, he had something like another mile to go. Say twenty minutes at the Appaloosa's walking pace, or maybe thirty, as the slope grew steeper and the ground beneath them turned to shale. No hurry. He preferred a steady, plodding progress over unfamiliar ground, particularly when its occupants might not be pleased to see him coming.

Had the chief or someone else in Tartarus forewarned the Gentiles working Lehi's claim that Rockwell planned to visit them?

Keeping a firm hand on the Sharps, he reckoned that he'd find out soon enough.

Rockwell had seen his share of mining operations, large and small. This one was somewhere in between, a shaft descending into darkness, but he couldn't say how far. Two rangy, dirty men were standing out in front of it and watching him approach. One held a pickaxe, while the other had a Colt Walker stuck through his belt for a left-handed draw. No move to pull it as Rockwell came up to them, edging the gelding around to his right, so the Sharps pointed midway between them.

"Marshal," said the one holding the pickaxe. He didn't look or sound surprised.

"Expecting me, were you?"

"Chief said you might be comin' out," the other said.

"You sure it was the chief?"

Both of them blinked at him. "I guess we oughta know Chief Fowler," Pickaxe said.

"So, not his doppelganger, then?"

"His double *what?*" Colt Walker asked.

Rockwell ignored him. Said, "Because I got the sense he rarely sticks a toe outside of town."

"I guess he gets around okay," said Pickaxe.

"Good to know. Who am I talking to?"

"Brett Murphy," Pickaxe said, then nodded to his left. "My brother, Clem."

"Two of you work this claim alone?"

"Mostly," said Clem. "Frien's help us out from time to time."

"That's nice of them. It's registered in your names, then, alone?"

Both of them squinted at him, looking for the trap. A longish minute passed before Brett answered back, "We got a couple of investors."

"Partners?"

"Well . . ."

"And who might they be?"

"Why you askin' us these questions?" Clem inquired.

"Chief didn't fill you in?"

"Just said you might be comin' out to talk about the Mormons," Brett replied.

"That's right, far as it goes."

"Where else you goin' with it, Marshal?"

"Anywhere it leads me, I suppose. About those partners . . ."

"I don't like ta say," Brett answered.

"Do it, anyhow."

They thought about defying him, but finally weren't up to it. "There's Mr. Beardsley," Clem allowed.

"Who is . . . ?"

"He runs saloons," Brett said. "Oh, yeah, and he's the mayor."

"Handy. Who else?"

"Who else?" Brett echoed him.

"You said *investors,* meaning more than one."

"Oh, right. There's Mr. Walton, justice of the peace. And Mr. Jacobs. Heads the Miner's League."

"That's all of them?"

"It is."

"No Seamus Hannigan?"

Clem laughed at that. "The pimp? Hell, no."

"So, how'd you come into this claim, exactly," Rockwell asked.

"The Mormons give it up," said Brett. "Reckon they didn't care for all the work involved."

Lie number one, for sure. "You say they *gave* it to you?"

"Sold it, what he means to say," Clem offered.

"For how much?"

"Five hunnert dollars." That from Brett.

"Five hundred for a played-out claim?"

"Played out?" Clem said. "Who told you—"

"They just *thought* it was played out," his brother interrupted. "We decided, why not take a chance."

"And your investors felt the same."

"Seems like."

"So, how's it doing for you?" Rockwell asked.

Another hesitation, then Brett told him, "Not too bad. I guess the Mormons just give up too soon."

"Some folks will do that. How about you let me see the bill of sale."

"Ain't here," Clem said.

"Where is it, then?"

"Guess Mr. Beardsley has it, back in town. He fronted half the price."

"He has the business savvy, does he?"

"Seems to, from the way he lives," Brett said.

"Maybe I'll have a word with him, at that. One other thing. These Mormons give you any notion where they might be headed, when they pulled up stakes?"

"We didn't talk about it none," said Clem. "They weren't like frien's or anything."

"You didn't get along with them?"

"Well . . ."

"They wanted money in a hurry," Brett explained. "No point us askin' where they's headed, was there?"

"Guess we'll see. You boys are generally here, I take it?"

"One of us, at least," said Clem. "It pays to keep a sharp eye on the claim."

"So I know where to find you, then."

"For what?" Brett asked him, sounding anxious.

Rockwell shrugged and said, "You never know."

He headed out, still riding north. One of them called to him, "Town's back the other way, ya know!"

"Thanks for the tip," he said, and passed on out of pistol range, beyond their line of sight.

He wasn't going back to Tartarus just yet. It stood to reason that he'd find another claim or two along that way, since someone had seen fit to clear a road of sorts. And sure enough, a half-mile's ride brought Rockwell to another shaft, no one outside to greet him this time, though he picked up voices echoing from somewhere underground.

He sat and waited for a good five minutes, then raised his voice. "Hello the mine!"

The muffled voices ceased, and Rockwell waited for a moment longer, then heard scuffling footsteps coming toward him from the darkness. Lantern light bobbed on the walls, then was extinguished on the edge of sunshine filtering beyond the adit. Two men finally emerged, one carrying a double-barreled shotgun, while the second held the lamp in his left hand, a shovel in his right. Again, Rockwell sat ready, with the Sharps angled in their general direction.

"Who'n hell are you?" the miner with the scattergun demanded.

"U.S. marshal," Rockwell answered. "Got a couple questions for you, if you have the time."

"And if we don't?"

"I've got a couple questions for you, anyway."

"Tha's what I figgered." Surly and resentful. "Ask away."

"You know the Murphy brothers, down the hill there?"

"More or less." It seemed that Shotgun did the talking. Fair enough.

"And what about the folks who had the claim before they got it?"

"Them? A buncha *Mormons*." Almost spitting out the word.

"You didn't cotton to them?"

"Cotton to a *Mormon?*" Shotgun sneered at the idea.

"I guess that means they didn't tell you why they planned on leaving?"

Shifty looks between the two, now, trying to conceal it. "Didn't tell us nothin'," Shotgun answered. "Weren't like we was *neighbors,* was it?"

"I suppose not. Never passed the time of day with them at all, coming or going?"

Shotgun shook his head, the very notion seeming foreign to him.

"Any idea how the claim's been doing since they left?"

"The hell would we know that?"

"Word gets around a mining town, when someone makes a strike."

"We don't know nothin' about *nothin'* but the work we do right here," Shotgun insisted.

"Right. Thanks for your time."

Instead of pushing any farther north, Rockwell decided he would likely hear some version of the same account from any miners he encountered in the neighborhood. He turned back southward, passed the Murphy claim without a glimpse of Brett or Clem, and kept on going downhill, winding back toward Tartarus. He had three other men to visit now, investors in the claim his nephew and the other Saints had chosen to abandon.

If, in fact, it was their choice.

Rockwell still wasn't sold on that, by any means, but he would give the men in charge of Tartarus a chance to sell him on the story first, before he judged them and considered how to shake the real truth loose. Sometimes it came without a fight, but other times . . .

The shot—a rifle's *crack*—came from behind him, somewhere higher up, and sent him plunging from his saddle to the ground.

CHAPTER 7

Rockwell lost his hat but hung onto his Sharps as he went down, hit hard, and rolled clear of the Appaloosa as it bolted from the sound of gunfire. Impact with the earth was jarring, but the shot had missed him, wasted. Now, before the sniper had a chance to try again, he wriggled under cover with a boulder at his back, shielding him from the slope above and to the west of him.

It wasn't much in terms of cover, granted. He was pinned down for the moment, and the man who'd tried to kill him—was there only one of them?—had full mobility to creep around and find another angle of attack. Rockwell was still considering his options when a second shot spanged off the boulder, whining into empty space and sprinkling him with slivers from the larger stone.

A rifle, once again. Likely the same one, from its sound, though Rockwell couldn't guarantee it. His first thought had been the Murphy brothers, but the only gun he'd seen in their possession was a pistol. And, so what? There had been time enough, after he left their claim, for one or both of them to run for long guns they'd kept hidden out of sight somewhere. More than enough time for them to climb up the ridge above their shaft and find a vantage point for dry gulching.

One thing that he could *not* afford to do was sit and wait for one or both of them to flank him. If they caught him in a crossfire, he was finished. The alternative, he knew, was to expose himself and take a chance.

Rockwell reared up, the Sharps against his shoulder, angling up the hillside. He was ready when the sniper fired again, black powder smoke betraying his position, with a huddled shape behind it. Rockwell fired off-hand and thought he saw a puff of crimson in the midst of all that smoke, but couldn't swear to it.

No matter. He was up and running in a heart-beat, empty rifle in his left hand, now, one of his Colts clutched in the right. The slope was steep and slippery, but Rockwell dug in with his boots, leaned into it, and willed himself to beat the pull of gravity. Somewhere above him, he was certain that he heard a cry of pain, perhaps a second voice responding to it, but the shooters missed their chance to pick him off while he was climbing, when he would have been a relatively easy mark. He stumbled, halfway to the summit, almost sliding back again, but he dropped the rifle, caught himself with his left hand, and charged ahead.

Cresting the rise gave them another chance to kill him, framed in silhouette against the sky, but there was no one left on top to do the job. Far off, and disappearing down a canyon, southward, Rockwell saw two horsemen, one slumped forward as if he was having trouble staying in the saddle.

Wounded?

Rockwell didn't try the Colt, since they were both well out of range. Long gone before he could have doubled back to fetch the Sharps, reload, and try to wing one of them on the run. He cursed and never gave a thought to asking Jesus for His pardon, focused now on finding out if he had scored a hit on either of his would-be killers.

And he found a patch of fresh blood on the ground, approximately where a wounded shooter would have fallen back, after he'd fired the Sharps uphill. The quantity was indeterminate, but no hit from a .52-caliber slug would qualify as minor. At the very least, it drilled a half-inch entrance wound, propelling mangled flesh before it. Even missing bones and vital organs, it would be a stunning wound, impact alone sufficient to take most men down and out.

If it had clipped a major artery or vein, the sniper was as good as dead.

It was too late to follow them. He had to scramble back downhill, retrieve his horse—and then, what?

Check the Murphy claim, for starters. His

intended killers had been riding south, toward Tartarus. If Brett and Clem were nowhere to be found, Rockwell would have a fair idea of who had ambushed him, and who had put them up to it.

Their three so-called investors. Beardsley. Walton. Jacobs.

And perhaps some more, besides.

The Appaloosa gelding came when Rockwell whistled for it, trotting up to him and standing ready while he took a moment to reload the Sharps. He mounted, then, and turned the animal back northward, thinking through the moves that lay ahead of him.

One way it could go, if the Murphys *were* the shooters, he would find their claim abandoned. No threat, there. Conversely, if the brothers weren't involved, they'd have no reason to be gunning for him. Yet another way to look at it, of course: they *were* involved, but hadn't fired the shots themselves—in which case, seeing Rockwell in the flesh might prod them into trying something on their own, impulsively.

Be ready, then, he thought. *Don't give them any slack.*

He didn't rush, returning to the Murphy claim, raking the slope above him and the drop-off to his right with narrowed eyes. Some fifty yards before he reached the shaft, Rockwell saw Brett and Clem out front, watching him ride their way. Clem had the Colt Walker still tucked under his belt, but Brett had left his pick somewhere and come out empty-handed.

"Heard some shootin'," Brett called out, when they were close enough to speak up without shouting.

"So did I," Rockwell replied. "Figured I'd better check and see if you were having trouble."

He couldn't read their faces clearly. If the brothers were surprised to see him breathing, they'd had time to mask it during his approach. Brett posed no threat to Rockwell at the moment, but he kept a closer eye on Clem, in case he started getting rattled and it drove him to a draw.

"No trouble here," Brett said. "Just gettin' back to work."

"I'm glad to hear it. If a wounded man turns up, you have the wherewithal to deal with him?"

"What wounded man?" Clem asked.

Rockwell allowed himself a shrug. "We all heard shooting. Stands to reason someone could be hit."

"Oh. Right."

"We ain't no doctors," Brett reminded him.

"You'd have some way to get him down the hill and into town, though?"

"Only got our mule," said Brett, and nodded vaguely toward the mine shaft.

"Oh, well. Don't fret about it," Rockwell said. "A man gets holed out here, he's likely done for, anyhow."

The brothers frowned in unison, Clem looking more confused than Brett. "You didn't see nobody when the shootin' started?" he inquired.

"Nary a soul," Rockwell replied. "You boys be safe now, hear?"

He left them chewing on it, holding off his smile until he'd turned his back on them and started down the dusty track toward level ground and Tartarus. Left them with something to consider, whether they had been involved in jumping him or not. Rockwell had no faith in coincidence, where killing was concerned, and seriously doubted that a pair of highwaymen would try picking him off by chance.

The answer, he felt confident, lay back in Tartarus. He didn't have enough to file a charge, by any means, but the attempt to kill him meant someone was scared enough to bet the limit. What they hadn't reckoned on was Rockwell's blessing from the Prophet, shielding him from any threat by mortal men.

Did he believe that? Was it literally true?

Why not?

Faith was the substance of things hoped for, and the evidence of things not seen. If he believed in Joseph Smith, the Holy Bible and the Book of Mormon—which he did—then nothing was impossible for God or His elect. How could he doubt the Prophet's power to invest a chosen warrior with invincibility?

Rockwell didn't think he was *immortal,* naturally. That would be ridiculous and contradictory of scripture. Hebrews spelled it out in no uncertain terms: it is appointed unto men once to die, but after this the judgment.

Rockwell knew that he would die, someday, but whether any mortal man could *kill* him was another question all together.

As for judgment, he was bringing it to Tartarus. He simply didn't know, yet, who would fall under the sword and which ones would be spared.

The town felt different to Rockwell as he entered it, the second time. Was he imagining an air of tension hanging over Main Street? An expectancy? The townsfolk passing up and down on either side all looked the same to him, first slightly curious, and then suspicious when they spied his badge. Rockwell ignored them, heading for the livery. The hostler greeted him and held his Appaloosa's reins as he dismounted.

"Any luck?" the old man asked.

"Not much. You have a sawbones here in town?"

"Sure do." The hostler looked concerned now, seemingly sincere. "You hurt or somethin'?"

"Just a question for him."

"Oh. Well, that'd be Doc Crowder, halfway down and on your left, next to the hardware store."

"Thanks. Can you go another night?"

"No trouble, Marshal. Long as you've a need."

From the hotel, dropping the Sharps off in his room, it was a short walk to the doctor's office, where a sign identified its occupant as Milton Crowder, M.D. It was supposed to be an office, so he didn't bother knocking, simply opening the door and stepping in. That set a small bell jangling overhead and brought a man of middle age from a backroom.

"Help you?"

"I'm looking for the doctor," Rockwell answered.

"And you've found him. Milton Crowder, at your service, Marshal."

Crowder was a man of average size, five-nine or -ten, around 180 pounds. He wore a vest over his white shirt, with the collar open. Striped trousers below, with shoes on small feet polished to a gleaming shine. His face was round and ruddy, with a thick moustache that matched his bushy eyebrows.

"What it is," Rockwell explained, "I'm looking for a wounded man."

"When you say wounded—"

"Shot."

"I see. So, you're not injured, then?"

"They missed," Rockwell replied.

"Thus, more than one."

"One hit. They both shinned out."

"And this happened today?"

"Within the past two hours."

"Well, sir, no one has required my services for any sort of wounds today."

"Thanks, anyway. Long shot, I guess." Then, almost as an afterthought, "You wouldn't have an undertaker in the neighborhood, by any chance?"

"We do," said Crowder. "Up a block, across the street. Marion Small."

"A woman undertaker?"

"No, sir. With an 'o' before the 'n,' it makes a man's name."

"Live and learn," said Rockwell, then he turned and passed into the street—where Rance Fowler met him on the sidewalk, looking startled.

"Marshal!"

"Chief."

"You're back."

"Looks like it."

Fowler flicked a glance in the direction of the doctor's office. "Any trouble?"

"None I couldn't handle."

"But you're talking to the doctor?"

"Nothing gets past you."

"I mean to say, if you're not hurt—"

"Somebody is," said Rockwell.

"Oh? You want to fill me in on that?"

"Outside your jurisdiction, Chief."

Fowler was clearly growing frustrated. "The Murphy brothers?"

"Nope. I left them safe and sound." Not tacking on, *For now.*

"Well, if you don't mind telling me . . ."

"Somebody bushwhacked me, out by their claim. I paid them back in kind."

"You tellin' me you shot at someone?"

"We've been over that."

"Awright, then, are you tellin' me you *shot* someone?"

"I got a piece of one. There were a couple of them."

"Not the Murrphys, though."

"I answered that already."

"And you thought the doctor might have seen them?"

Rockwell shrugged. "They headed this way, riding out. I took it as a possibility, unless they stopped off somewhere in between."

"No spreads to speak of out that way," said Fowler. "Only mining claims."

"Narrows it down. I'm talking to your undertaker next."

"Uh-huh. Well, I suppose I'll leave you to it, then."

"Before you go, Chief, I'll be looking for some of your people here."

"Which people?" Wary now.

"Your mayor. Justice of the peace. Head of your miner's league."

Fowler wore the expression of a man who'd stepped in something rank. "Why them, for heaven's sake?"

"I'll lay that out for them in person. What I need from you is how to find them."

"Well, um . . . Mr. Beardsley's got an office at the Lucky Strike. You woulda passed it, ridin' in."

"The others?"

"Mr. Walton runs the assay office. Mr. Jacobs works the Plata Belleza mine, west of town. Means somethin' in Mexican, he claims."

"Silver Beauty," said Rockwell.

"You speak their lingo?"

"West of town, that was?"

"Uh-huh."

"Looks like I'll need another of your maps."

"Oh. Well . . ."

"You need another pencil?"

"Reckon I still got one in the office."

"I'll just walk down with you, then."

"Okay." Chief Fowler didn't seem enthused about it.

"Funny," Rockwell said, as they were walking back to Fowler's office.

"What is?"

"Someone jumping me, when I went out to see the Murphy boys."

"This is a wild neck of the woods, I won't deny it."

"All outside your jurisdiction, though."

"Well."

"It may be lucky that I get to meet your undertaker."

"How's that lucky, Marshal?"

"Hey, you never know. I might be throwing him some business pretty soon."

Marion Small was more or less as advertised— a short man, though not dwarfish. Say a foot shorter than Rockwell, give or take a quarter-inch. He had the solemn look that seems to be a standard for the trade, like black frock coats, string ties, and shiny trousers. This one's eyes were even tombstone gray, which seemed to fit. The only color anywhere about him was the shock of red hair covering his scalp, extending into bushy muttonchops. His skin was pale behind that hair, his roly-poly figure testifying to a measure of prosperity. The undertaker's parlor smelled of flowers, although there were none in evidence.

Small greeted Rockwell with a handshake, heard him out, nodding along the way, then said, "I'm sorry I can't help you, Marshal. No one's been brought in to me today."

"Well, if you get a call—"

"I'll let you know at once, of course. You say you're staying at the Grand Hotel?"

"That's what they call it."

"Are you not impressed with the amenities?"

"Beats sleeping on the ground," Rockwell allowed.

"I should imagine so. Will you be staying long?"

"A while, yet. Let me ask you something."

"Certainly."

"What have you heard about the Mormon claim, as was, out north of town."

"Mormon?"

"A group from Salt Lake City. It's the Murphy claim today, they tell me."

"Ah. Then I'm afraid I have to disappoint you once again. My only contact with the miners is in a professional capacity."

"When they're toes-up, you mean."

"Correct."

"Most of your deaths are natural, I take it?"

"Most," Small said. "Not all, by any means. The town and its vicinity are somewhat . . . unsophisticated, shall we say?"

"I got that feeling, too. You've seen your share of killings, then."

"Regrettably."

"Claim-jumpers and the like?"

"A few. Most of the homicides come out of the saloons."

"Police clear most of those?"

"There's rarely any prosecution. Fighting over

cards or women. Most of them go down as self-defense."

"Would you agree with that?"

Small frowned. "I leave that to the courts."

"Meaning the miner's court, or Mr. Walton?"

"That depends on jurisdiction, I suppose."

"It would," Rockwell agreed. "And you'd have known if any Mormons cycled through your shop here, either natural or otherwise disposed of."

"Most assuredly."

"All right. Thanks, anyway."

"I'm happy to assist you, Marshal."

Which you didn't, Rockwell thought, but let it go. Standing outside of Small's establishment, he made a mental list of things to do. Lunch first, because his stomach had begun to grumble at him, which would mean another visit to Delmonico's. From there, he could decide whether to call on Mayor Beardsley first, or drop in on the justice of the peace. He didn't feel like riding out to see another mine just now, and put that off until tomorrow, if he hadn't dug up anything in Tartarus.

He had a steak in mind, or maybe stew if it was on the menu. Food was just about the only thing he couldn't criticize so far, in Tartarus—that, and the livery. He didn't trust the people any farther than he could have thrown his Appaloosa. Fowler, he believed, possessed some kind of guilty knowledge, but he couldn't pin it down.

Rockwell imagined he would have a better take on what was happening after he'd spoken to the Murphy brothers' various investors and discovered how the Mormon claim came up for sale.

Although he had a fairly good idea.

Jumping to a conclusion, Rockwell understood from prior experience, was perilous. Hasty decisions put himself at risk, along with others who might suffer injury. His best bet was to gather all the facts available, see where they led, then choose a course of action suited to the circumstances.

He was moving toward Delmonico's, passing along the west side of the street, when someone called out to him from a shadowed alleyway. No, that was wrong. It hadn't been a call to *him,* specifically, more of a bleating cry for help. A woman's voice, although he couldn't make out what she'd said and wasn't even certain that the words were English.

Putting away his thoughts of food, Rockwell turned to his right and stepped into the alley's mouth.

CHAPTER 8

Three ruffians had trapped a woman there, well back from Main Street, and were shoving her around between themselves, playing some kind of game that Rockwell took to be a prelude to the violation they intended. All of them were burly, of a decent size, though not his height. Their chortling laughter told him they were drunk, but nowhere close to passing out.

Too bad.

As Rockwell closed the gap, the woman turned in his direction, sobbing, blouse torn down the front, and he could see she was Chinese. *Celestial,* the press and common lingo dubbed them, not because they were presumed to come from some far distant world among the stars, but because their emperors referred to China as the Celestial Empire.

Here, in the United States and its territories, Celestial numbers were growing by leaps and bounds. Rockwell had read somewhere that there were fewer than four hundred in the whole of North America when Brigham Young had led the Saints to Deseret. Today, by all accounts, thirty thousand or more were employed in mining, building railroads, or huddled together in Chinese quarters of cities ranging nationwide, from San

Francisco to New York. Rockwell had seen their laundry boiling sheets in Tartarus, and now he was confronted with a female of the species in distress.

He had a choice to make: move on and let the thugs amuse themselves, or intervene.

His badge and Christian duty took the choice away from Rockwell. Scowling at the turn his luck had taken, he advanced.

"Well now," he said to no one in particular. "What have we here?"

The three men paused, one of them hanging on to each of the young woman's arms, all facing Rockwell now. Drunk as they were, despite the shade, they saw and recognized his badge.

"Nothin' for you to be concerned about, Marshal," the nearest of them said. "A little fun, is all."

"It doesn't look like fun to her," Rockwell replied.

"This little China gal? She don't mind none." The second speaker clutched her left arm, giving her a strong shake as he slurred his words.

"I guess she's crying tears of joy, then," Rockwell said.

"She *will* be, in a minute," said the third man. "You could always stay and get yourself a piece."

"I'd rather that you let her go and walk away."

"An' what if'n we don't?" the first man asked him.

"Then your undertaker stands to have his work cut out for him."

Two of the men were wearing pistols, while the third carried both a revolver and a hunting knife. Despite the odds, Rockwell was not particularly worried. They were drunk, and he suspected none of them had benefited from a prophet's blessing of invincibility.

"You wanna try all three of us?" the gunman to the woman's right inquired, grinning.

"Wouldn't be my first choice," Rockwell answered. "But I've shot one man today, already. I could just as easy make it four."

"The hell you say," their seeming leader growled.

"Hell's where you're going, if you pull that smoke pole."

With a snarl, their front man fumbled at his pistol in its low-slung holster. Rockwell drew one of his Navy Colts and shot the drunk as near dead center as he could, swinging around to face the others as the first one dropped. They'd both released the woman by that time, gaping at Rockwell for a second, then broke off in opposite directions, going for their guns.

The alley worked against them, keeping them from dodging out of range or finding any cover. Rockwell took the shooter on his left first, since he'd turned a bit in that direction for the first one anyway. His second shot was low, drilling the would-be rapist's gut, letting the wind out of him in a howl of pain as he collapsed.

That still left one, the slowest of the trio, with his pistol barely clearing leather. Rockwell covered him and said, "Be sure you want to go this way."

The drunk froze, thinking through it in a haze of fear and alcohol, then went ahead. Rockwell released a pent-up sigh and shot him in the face, skimming his old hat off behind him, spattering the nearby wall with gray and scarlet.

Sharp echoes from the alley rattled into Main Street, bringing morbid gawkers to observe the scene. Before they gathered, though, the Chinese girl was gone, escaping from the far end of the alley, ducking to her left and out of Rockwell's sight.

He waited for the chief, reloading while he stood there, watching townsfolk watching him. It took Fowler the best part of ten minutes to arrive, but Rockwell's gut-shot adversary still had life left in him yet, though maybe not for long.

"What in pluperfect hell is *this* about?" the chief demanded.

Rockwell summarized it for him, kept it short, if not exactly sweet. Fowler surveyed the carnage and inquired, "So what's become of the Celestial?"

"Ran off," Rockwell replied. "Seems natural, under the circumstances."

"Can you give me a description of her?"

"Young. Chinese."

"That don't help much."

"Yon fat one got a better look at her than I did. Maybe he can tell you, if you get him to the doc in time."

"Reckon he'll tell it your way?" Fowler asked.

"That's not my problem."

"Could be, though. Stranger in town who's shot four people."

"Five," Rockwell corrected him. "I'm still looking for one."

"You treat that badge of yours like it's a huntin' license."

"What else do you call it? These three were about to rape a woman, and they pulled on me. Maybe you'd rather stand around and jaw with them."

"They're *white* men, dammit!"

"You'd excuse them, then?"

"Well, I—"

"Because I never heard that evil had a color to it."

Fowler's cheeks had taken on some color of their own. "You plan on staying here in Tartarus much longer, Marshal?"

"Till I'm finished with the job that I was sent to do."

"By Brigham Young?"

"You have a problem with the governor," said Rockwell, "take it up with him. Meanwhile, if you're not helping me, the best thing you can do is stay out of my way."

"Another threat?"

"Remember what I told you about that."

Rockwell reversed direction, striding toward the east end of the alley. Fowler called after him, "Where are you goin' now?"

Under his breath, Rockwell replied, "To get my laundry done."

It was not difficult to find the Chinese quarter in a town the size of Tartarus. Rockwell knew where the laundry was and calculated they would dwell in close proximity. Approaching from behind it, rather than the Main Street entrance, he saw twenty-odd Celestials standing together, watching him approach with hostile eyes in faces otherwise devoid of all emotion.

Rockwell didn't know which ones spoke English, but he figured some must, if they managed to do business with the other folks in town. He tried it, telling them, "I'm looking for the girl who had some trouble up the street, there. It's been taken care of, and I'd like to see if she's all right."

Some muttering he couldn't translate, then a man older than those ranged out in front of him stepped forward, easing through their ranks, the young men parting silently. "You are not one of Chief Fowler's men," he said.

"No, sir. I'm not."

"His men would not have helped my grand-daughter."

Granddaughter? Rockwell thinking this could work to his advantage if he handled it correctly.

"Well, it seemed the Christian thing to do," he said.

"Christian?" The old man's frown was in his voice, not on his face. "You are . . . unusual."

"I've heard it said."

"I am in debt to you."

"Well, if you feel that way, I've got a question for you."

After due consideration, the old man said, "Ask it."

"I've been sent to find out what became of certain people hereabouts," Rockwell explained. "Prospectors and their wives. They worked a claim, out north of town, but now they've gone away without a word to anyone they knew, back home."

The old man talked with some of his people for a while, in their own singsong language, then he said, "You mean the different ones."

Rockwell considered that, then nodded. "I expect that's right."

"We had no dealings with them," said the

97

old man. "They did not bring clothes to us for cleaning, but we saw them sometimes. They remained apart from those you see today. No whores or whiskey. Careful with their speech and with their women."

"Sounds like who I'm looking for."

"You come too late," the old man said.

"How's that?"

"You understand that we saw nothing. But we listen when the round-eyes think we do not understand."

"I'll take what I can get," Rockwell replied. "Were these ones friends of yours?"

"I knew a couple of them. One was kin to me. My family."

The old man nodded solemnly. "One day, about two months ago, they all come into town. Go to the assay office, come out happy. Go to stores, come out with things. After they leave, Chief Fowler meets with other men."

"Beardsley and Walton?" Rockwell asked, trying his luck.

"You know them?"

"Haven't had the pleasure, but I aim to. Maybe they brought in a fellow by the name of Jacobs?"

"I do not know that one. First the three meet, then more come and go. One night, they have a celebration at the Lucky Strike. We do not see your friends again."

"That's all you heard?"

"A few nights later, two men drunk on Main Street talk and laugh about Mormons. You understand this lingo?"

"I can work it out all right."

"Some of the other men, later, bring bloody clothes to wash."

Rockwell had been anticipating this, but even so, it felt like stones had settled in his stomach. Lehi and the others, absolutely gone and never coming back. He still had work to do, more digging, but the old man had removed whatever fleeting doubt he might have harbored that the Saints had simply given up and left their diggings without looking back.

"Appreciate the help," he told the old man. "And I'll do my best to see that none of this lands back on you."

"How will you punish them?"

"I've not decided yet," said Rockwell. "But you'll know it when I start."

"A *Chinese* girl?" Paul Beardsley looked confused. "The hell's he doin', here?"

"Maybe it struck him wrong," said Fowler. "Three on one. Who knows?"

"Mormons are odd," said Isaac Walton. "Marry all the wives they want, but won't touch liquor. Don't want anybody else to have a little fun."

"These men he smoked," said Beardsley. "Were they anybody?"

99

"Had a claim they call the Glory Hole, out east of town," Fowler replied.

"Survivors?"

"If the one he gut-shot makes it."

"We should take a look at that. Make him an offer," Walton said.

"Unless he croaks," said Beardsley. "Wouldn't cost us nothin', then."

"Before you get distracted," Fowler interjected, "what about ol' Rockwell."

"Why don't you arrest him?"

Fowler snorted. "He as good as told me that he'd liketa see me try it."

"That's defiance of the law, right there," said Walton.

"Overlookin' that he has a U.S. badge, hisself."

"He's shot four men," Walton replied.

"*Five* men," Beardsley corrected him. "Lou didn't make it, by the way."

"God*damn*." Fowler slumped back into his chair, shaking his head. "I ain't about to tackle Porter Rockwell. You can take my badge and—"

"Simmer down," said Beardsley. "No one's askin' you to sacrifice yourself."

"Although you *might* consider offering a little public service," Walton interjected.

"I already *did* that," Fowler said. "I covered up *your* tracks."

"Now, see here—"

"Rance! Isaac!" Beardsley's voice cut through

their bickering. "If we can't stick together, we're as good as done for."

Fowler bristled. "I'm just sayin'—"

"You already *said* it. What we need to do, right now, is put our heads together and decide what happens next."

"What happens," Fowler said, "is that he keeps on sniffin' till he finds somethin' to hang us with."

"Maybe. But only if we let it go that far."

"You tried to kill him twice," Fowler replied. "Seems like it didn't work too well."

"I hardly count the time with Hannigan," said Beardsley. "Lou and Jake, I will admit, were disappointments to me."

"Think how Lou must feel."

"That's funny, Chief. You oughta be a comic on the stage."

"I just meant—"

"Where is he now?" Beardsley cut into his apology. "I mean, right now."

"Delmonico's," said Fowler.

"Shooting people doesn't spoil his appetite, I guess," said Walton.

"Shouldn't," Fowler said. "From what I hear, he's done enough of it."

"He's damn sure done enough in Tartarus," said Beardsley. "And I want it stopped."

"Okay, but how?" asked Fowler.

"Where'd you say he's goin' next?"

"To see the pair of you."

Walton leaned forward in his chair, closer to Beardsley. "If he comes in here, you've got him, Paul."

"How do you figure that?"

"We all know people have a tendency to disappear when you get tired of 'em."

"Just drunks and drifters, now and then a miner winnin' more than he's entitled to at faro."

"All the same."

"It *ain't* the same. Rockwell's a U.S. marshal. He can't walk in here and disappear."

"Why not? Who's ever gonna say he *did* walk in?"

"There's always somebody. The next marshal shows up, or maybe more than one, they'll sniff around till they shake somethin' loose."

"So, what's your plan?"

"Let Jacobs handle it."

"How's that?" asked Fowler.

"Simple. He comes to either one of us, we point him toward Emil at the Plata Belleza."

"Silver Beauty," Fowler muttered to himself.

"What's that?"

"I gave Rockwell the name. He told me what it means in Mexican."

"Spanish," Walton corrected him.

"Whichever. Anyway, how's Jacobs know to deal with him if he rides out there."

"*When* he rides out. Someone needs to go out

first and talk to Emil. Let him know what's goin' on."

"Who's doin' that?" asked Fowler.

"You are, Chief."

"But that's—"

"Don't tell me it's outside your jurisidiction, Rance. I have to wait around till Rockwell comes to see me. Same for Isaac."

"Send one of your boys," Fowler suggested.

"Why not just go up and down the street askin' for volunteers?" Beardsley suggested, sneering. "I'd prefer to keep it private, if you don't mind."

"Sure. Okay."

"And on your way back, fetch the Murphy brothers into town."

"What for?"

"Because I said so!" Beardsley snapped at him, then softened. "Anything goes wrong at Emil's place, I want 'em here. They done good work for us with Mormons last time 'round, remember. If they wanna keep their share, they need to help us clean this up."

"Okay."

"You'd best get goin'."

Fowler had another thought. "Suppose he sees me headin' out?"

"What if he does? You got a right to take a ride, don't you?"

"I guess that's right."

"It's time you grew a backbone, Chief."

"Uh-huh." The insult warmed Fowler's cheeks.

"And come straight back here when you're done," said Beardsley.

"With the Murphys," he replied. "Awright."

"Hell, no! Don't bring 'em back here with you. Have 'em ride in on their own, for God's sake."

"Okay. Right."

"Like talkin' to a kid, I swear," Beardsley was saying, as he closed the office door.

Fowler was sick of being bullied and talked down to, but he couldn't think of anything to do about it. He was stuck—in Tartarus, behind the useless badge he wore, under Paul Beardsley's thumb. Most of the townsfolk treated him like he was nothing but a stooge, and Fowler couldn't blame them. He was no more cut out for a lawman's job than he was fit for surgery or teaching school. Sometimes he sat and wondered what he *was* fit for, and wound up drinking when he couldn't think of any decent answers.

Serve them right if I rode out and kept on going, Fowler thought. But then, what would he do? Where would he go? Not Salt Lake City, after this. Maybe head west, to California, or south, into New Mexico. Why not keep going all the way, while he was at it, into Mexico itself? A man could lose himself down there, maybe forget what he was running from if he put down enough tequila.

Maybe Porter Rockwell wouldn't find him there.

He knew that Beardsley was mistaken, thinking they could kill a U.S. marshal and their trouble would evaporate. It might be weeks before the hammer fell, but Fowler had no doubt that it *would* fall. He'd heard the stories: Rockwell and the governor; the Danites, Brigham Young's "Avenging Angels." Some said all of that was hogwash, fairy tales to frighten children, but Rance Fowler wasn't sure. Someone had obviously shot the governor—ex-governor, whatever—in Missouri, and it seemed to him that Rockwell hadn't quite denied it, after all. Then, there was Mountain Meadows, better than a hundred dead, and *that* was no damn fairy tale.

Clear out, a voice said, in his mind. And then another answered back, *Too late.*

He'd cast his lot with Beardsley and the others, took the path of least resistance when he could have cut and run with hands still clean. Now, any way he sliced it, Fowler reckoned that he had to stay and face whatever happened next.

And hope that he came out of it alive.

CHAPTER 9

Rockwell ate steak with all the trimmings at Delmonico's, then headed for the Lucky Strike to find Mayor Beardsley. Pushing through the bat-wing doors, he was assaulted by the too-familiar smell of every saloon he'd ever visited: tobacco smoke and alcohol, stale sweat and desperation. He moved past gaming tables, most of them unoccupied at that hour, and went directly to the bar.

"What'll you have, Marshal?" the barkeep asked.

"Your boss," Rockwell replied.

"Don't know if he's around."

"It shouldn't be much trouble finding out."

"I'm kinda busy here, right now."

"All right. I'll just go back and have a look around, myself."

"Hang on, now. Lemme check the office."

Rockwell waited for a good two minutes, then the bartender came back wearing a sour expression on his homely face. He cocked a thumb over his shoulder, toward a doorway at the far end of the bar, to Rockwell's left, and said, "He'll see you. Go on back."

The arching doorway could have been a trap, but Rockwell risked it, stepping through into a hallway that ran on for thirty feet or so, with closed doors lining either side. The first door on his right was labeled OFFICE—PRIVATE. Rockwell knocked and waited for a deep voice on the other side to say, "Come in!"

A reasonably tall man stood behind a desk piled high with money. Rockwell spotted gold coins minted by the federal government, others stamped by mining companies, and stacks of multicolored paper currency emblazoned with the names of banks that issued them. There was no standard paper currency for the United States at large, but rather notes printed by sixteen hundred private banks from coast to coast, some thirty thousand different colors and designs in all.

"Looks like you do all right," Rockwell allowed.

"I'm getting by," the boss man said, coming around his desk, right hand extended. "You'd be Marshal Rockwell."

"And I take it you're the mayor?"

"Paul Beardsley."

Rockwell pumped his hand once, then released it. "You're a man of many parts, I understand."

"A businessman, that's all. I try'n make a profit where I can."

"Saloons and such."

"In part."

"And mining claims?"

"I've got a few. You'd be surprised what some

men wager when they're drawing to an inside straight. You want to have a seat?"

"I won't be here that long."

"Quick business, then. What's on your mind."

"The Murphy claim, out north of town."

"I'd need to hear a little more."

"They tell me you're one of their backers."

"Do they, now?"

Rockwell let silence answer that one, waiting out the mayor. When it began to grow uncomfortable, Beardsley said, "I did provide some funding there, along with others."

"Like your justice of the peace."

"As an investment. Think of us as silent partners."

"What I'm interested in is how the first folks on the claim happened to sell."

"Why ask me?"

"It struck me that the Murphys were a mite confused about the sale, what prompted it and all. Their story doesn't jibe with what Chief Fowler told me, come to that."

"Not sure I follow," Beardsley said.

"One side tells me the claim played out, another says the people working it got tired of all the work and just moved on. You see my difficulty."

"Well . . ."

"And then I hear a rumor that the folks who filed the first claim never left at all."

Beardsley was frowning now. "Who told you that?"

Rockwell ignored him. Said, "Meaning, as I was led to understand, that something might have happened to them that would leave the mining operation up for grabs."

" 'Fraid you're beyond me now, Marshal."

"Claim jumping's what I had in mind."

"Uh-huh. I wouldn't know a damn thing about that."

"The Murphys come to you for money, but they never mentioned anything about their claim to someone else's property?"

"I put some money up, is all. I never saw a bill of sale, only the paperwork drawn up to certify my share."

"Of anything they find."

"That's it."

"And I suppose your Mr. Walton has the same perspective."

"Never held a pick or shovel in his life, that I know of."

"Or talked to any Mormons about selling out their claim?"

"Know who might help you there, and I say *might*. You oughta have a word with Emil Jacobs."

"Chairman of the Miner's League," said Rockwell. "At the Silver Beauty mine."

"The very same."

"Another partner."

"But more direct, though," Beardsley said. "Some of his boys go help the Murphys out from time to time."

"Thanks for the tip."

"I try to help the law whenever possible."

Rockwell let that one go, was turning toward the door when Beardsley said, "You'll keep me posted? On whatever you find out?"

"Won't be a secret," Rockwell said, and closed the office door behind him as he left.

His next stop, after seeing Beardsley, was the Grand Hotel. He used the privy in the yard out back, then went upstairs. The room was undisturbed from when he'd left it last. Rockwell retrieved his Sharps, the bandolier and tomahawk, then headed back downstairs. The clerk, not present when he'd entered, had returned from somewhere and was fidgeting behind his counter.

"Marshal Rockwell! Are you leaving us?"

"Just for an hour or two."

"Further investigation?"

"Thought I'd do some hunting."

"Hunting?"

"Try my luck, you know."

"With deer, or . . . what, particularly?"

"Anything that makes a run for it."

"Well . . . would you care to book another night?"

"Looks like it."

"Excellent." A show of false enthusiasm if he'd ever seen one. "I'll just note that in the register."

"Nobody's left you any word about those missing miners, I suppose."

"The Mormons? Sorry, no."

"Well, nothing ventured."

From the Grand Hotel, he walked down to the livery. The hostler looked surprised to see him for a second time that day. "Takin' another ride?" he asked.

"Seems like I can't sit still."

"Well, I'll just get him saddled up for you."

Riding out of Tartarus, westbound, Rockwell thought it was even money that he would be ambushed either on the road, or at the Silver Beauty mine. If so, he'd know the order came from Beardsley, in collaboration with the claim's other investors. And from there . . . what?

If he collected solid evidence of claim-jumping and murder, Rockwell had authority to round up those responsible and take them back for trial in Salt Lake City's federal court. In fact, however, that might not be feasible, considering the fact that his prime suspects were the leading citizens of Tartarus, with an uncertain number of supporters to defend them. Realistically, he'd need a good-sized posse to begin making arrests, and by the time he organized a raiding party, Beardsley and the others might be long gone into California, Oregon, New Mexico—wherever.

Or, they might dig in and make a fight of it, in which case Rockwell stood to lose his posse and his life. But if they only had to deal with one man, working on his own, the other side might start to make mistakes.

Like taking it for granted that he'd be an easy kill.

They'd muffed that once, already. Maybe twice, if one-eyed Seamus Hannigan was doing Beardsley's bidding with his bungled badger game. The three drunks with the Chinese girl were on their own, he thought. No way for them to know when he'd be passing by their alley, if at all, or whether he'd concern himself with their shenanigans.

Whatever else they had in mind, he took for granted that the claim's investors still had shooters left to throw at him. He hoped so, anyway.

It made what he was planning easier—assuming he survived.

The road leading him west from Tartarus was little different from the one he'd followed northward to the Murphy claim, that morning. Steeper, it was, rising higher into the Independence Range, but otherwise the scenery was more or less identical, winding across the Owyhee Desert with its sage, cactus, and Joshua trees, volcanic rock unyielding to the Appaloosa's hooves. Above Rockwell, the hills and buttes supported scattered whitebark pines, the tallest of them standing sixty feet or so. The wind was cold over a light dusting of snow, which meant no rattlesnakes to watch for, but he wasn't worried about reptiles.

Not the scaly kind, at least.

It would be difficult—maybe impossible—for Beardsley to alert buddy Jacobs that a visitor was coming, in the time since Rockwell had stopped by the Lucky Strike. That did not mean they hadn't worked it out beforehand, though. Call it a hedge against the failure of their first attempt to kill him, earlier that day.

An ace up Beardsley's sleeve, in case he needed one.

Rockwell had never played a hand of poker in his life, but he knew about betting the limit—in this case, his life. And there was one thing Beardsley should have guessed.

He didn't bluff.

Rance Fowler was uneasy on his ride out to the Murphy claim. He didn't like the thought of running into Rockwell outside town, although he thought the odds of that were slim, since Paul had pointed him toward Emil Jacobs, west of Tartarus. Aside from that, the open country made him nervous. Cougars in the hills, and hostile Indians to boot.

As if the Murphy boys alone weren't bad enough.

Why Beardsley had selected them as front men for the Mormon claim was anybody's guess. Fowler had never asked him, didn't care to know. That was the least of his concerns, if word of what had happened to the so-called Saints got back to Brigham Young in Salt Lake City. There'd be hell to pay, and as the man who was supposed to be the law in Tartarus, Fowler would be the first one up to answer for it. Beardsley damn sure wouldn't hang around to share the blame, or Walton. They could pull up stakes at any time, with all the loot they had accumulated; same for Jacobs, if he felt like cutting loose his Silver Beauty claim.

Not me, thought Fowler. *I don't have a pot to—*

"Chief!" a voice cut through his sour reverie. "What brings you out this way?"

Fowler looked up to see Brett Murphy looming over him, a Colt revolving rifle braced against his hip. He had the same sneer on his face as usual, mistaking arrogance for courage.

"You'n Clem are wanted back in town," said Fowler.

"Oh? Says who?"

"The mayor. You wanna snub him, I'll be happy to inform him."

"Hey, I never said that!"

"Then collect your brother and get moving."

114

Fowler was already turning from the youngster, on his grullo mare, when Murphy called down to him, "This about that marshal? What's his name, again?"

"Rockwell. The mayor will tell you anything you need to know."

"What'sa matter, Chief? He got you in the dark?"

"Right where I wanna be," Fowler replied, "when this one sticks his nose in."

"Me'n Clem ain't skeert of him."

"Keep sayin' that," Fowler called back over his shoulder. "Maybe you'll believe it when you need to."

Murphy cursed him, then retreated. Fowler heard the hothead's boots scrabbling on stone, going to fetch his brother for the trip to town. He wondered which of them would ride their mule, or whether they'd take turns. If they kept Beardsley waiting too long, it would mean a scolding, nothing they'd enjoy. Not Fowler's problem, though he wouldn't mind watching Beardsley deliver that tongue-lashing, bring the brothers down a peg or two.

Feed them to Rockwell, and how long would either of them last? Not long, in Fowler's estimation, but you never knew. A green kid could get lucky, every now and then. Fowler imagined that the mayor meant to hold them in reserve, together with the hard men from his several saloons, in case Rockwell got past the Jacobs bunch.

Not likely, he imagined, then he thought about the havoc that the Mormon marshal had already wreaked in Tartarus, and Fowler wasn't quite so sure. Jacobs had six or seven men out at the Silver Beauty mine, all fairly decent hands with guns. Taken together, that should be enough to bed down any man.

But Porter Rockwell *wasn't* any man. He might have tried to kill a governor, for pity's sake, and rumor had it that he stacked up ordinary men like cord wood. Three so far, in Tartarus, with one more dying slow while Milton Crowder tried to keep him comfy. The only one to walk away from him so far—well, *limp* away—was Seamus Hannigan, and you could say his dancing days were over.

It was a cold ride back to town, but Fowler had one consolation, anyway. The Murphy brothers weren't along to goad him with their smart mouths all the way. He thought about them standing up to Rockwell, going down together, and it almost made him smile.

Almost.

Until he thought about the Mormon marshal coming after him.

The map Fowler had drawn for Rockwell wasn't what you'd call precise. It gave a sense of scale and distance, with a fair take on direction, and he thought that he was getting closer, but he couldn't say if it would be another thirty minutes or an hour, maybe more. Still not a long ride, by his normal standards, but he wanted to be done with it.

Get down to business.

Rockwell knew what had become of Lehi and the other Saints who'd come with him to Tartarus. He couldn't say where they were planted and might never know, but they were dead, all right. Paul Beardsley and his partners were responsible, although he doubted they had personally joined in any of the bloodletting. The only question nagging at him now was *who else* knew about the murders. Who participated in the killings? Who covered them up? Who all had profited in any way from the annihilation of nine men and women, none of whom had posed a threat of any kind to Tartarus?

The whole town, maybe. In which case, he just might have to wipe it off the map.

Paul Beardsley's lead to Emil Jacobs smelled like what it likely was: a trap. That didn't worry Rockwell, in itself. He was used to taking risks, weighing the odds whenever possible, but forging on regardless if his cause was just. With any luck, he might learn something from the owner of the Silver Beauty mine—or from his men, at least, if Jacobs liked to keep his own hands clean.

Talk first, if possible, before the shooting started.

Then again, what if he had it wrong? What if Mayor Beardsley hadn't tipped his partner off to Rockwell stopping by? Maybe the man in charge of Tartarus was setting Jacobs up to be his straw man, or a sacrificial goat to clear the rest of them. Let Jacobs bear the brunt of Rockwell's wrath, then claim he tricked his partners into buying shares after the dirty deed was done without their knowledge.

Rockwell couldn't swallow that, but it was something that a jury might accept if fancy lawyers pled the case and got them tangled up in legal jargon, while their clients looked contrite and wept crocodile tears.

Could anything along those lines be true?

Rockwell believed himself a fairly decent judge of character, and he had pegged Paul Beardsley as a liar from the moment that they met. He looked and smelled like a confidence man, maybe raised as a nipper, a man with no scruples beyond looking out for himself. His bright smile was an oily counterfeit. Rockwell would lose no sleep over eliminating him, as long as he made sure he had the right of it.

Another mile, he thought. Even the bumbling chief who rarely left his small-town jurisdiction couldn't be much farther off than that.

He would be ready with his Sharps on the

approach, and with his Colts—his Bowie and the tomahawk as well, if it came down to that. A newspaper reporter in Missouri had described him as a savage once, and Rockwell wouldn't quarrel with that when he was fighting for his life. The only rule in gunfighting, or combat hand to hand, was to survive. Whatever was required to come out of the fray alive, was justified.

And much the same, he thought, for settling accounts.

His nephew and the others had been slaughtered out of hand, as Rockwell saw it, for their silver. That was murder, robbery, and an affront to God's own congregation. One way he could look at it was standing back, letting Paul Beardsley and the others sow their oats and profit from their crimes until the Lord called them before His judgment seat some years or decades hence.

But Rockwell didn't have that kind of patience. What he had was an assignment, and a duty—to the dead, the governor, and to himself—to put things right. Balance the scales on earth, and leave the afterlife to Someone else.

A reckoning.

First, he would meet with Emil Jacobs, listen to the chairman of the Miners' League and find out where that took him. Whatever happened after that was down to Rockwell's adversaries. They could always choose surrender, travel back to

Salt Lake City with him, take their chances in a courtroom.

But he didn't think they would.

And that—why not admit it to himself, at least?—would suit him fine.

CHAPTER 10

Emil Jacobs cut a short plug of tobacco, wedged it into his left cheek, then returned the rest to its pouch and the pouch to his pocket. Facing east, toward Tartarus, he saw a solitary rider drawing closer, not in any hurry from his pace, but clearly headed for the Plata Belleza digs.

Silver Beauty.

There wasn't much beauty to mining, but Jacobs did admire the ore his workers pried out of the ground. More than its luster, he enjoyed the wealth it brought to him, a simple farmer's son who had decided scratching at the ground to raise a crop was foolish, if the same amount of work could get him precious ore. These days, he didn't even have to do the work himself.

Was this a great country, or what?

But now he and his partners had a situation on their hands. It was a problem of their own creation, granted, but they'd given in to greed and that was done, no way to take it back. Jacobs had made his choice, along with Beardsley, Walton, and the rest. He had to live with it, and living was exactly what he meant to do. He didn't plan on climbing any scaffold, praying that he wouldn't soil himself in front of strangers when the trap sprang open and he plummeted through space, a noose around his neck.

This had to be the marshal coming, Porter Rockwell, said to be the meanest Danite in the private army Brigham Young had organized to deal with enemies of his religion. Jacobs didn't care much what a man believed, as long as he was smart enough to live and let live, without trying to impose his creed on anybody else.

The problem with this Rockwell was the U.S. badge he wore, and what it symbolized. If he was killed, or simply disappeared, Jacobs knew other marshals would eventually come to find out what became of him. That was a problem for another day, however. He could only deal with trouble as it came and do his best to make it go away.

He walked back to the mine shaft's entrance, shouting down into the darkness, "Boys! I need you topside, pronto!"

In another moment, Jacobs heard them scrabbling toward him, following the lead man with his lamp, like trolls emerging from their cave. The first man out, Vic Tunney, was his foreman, asking, "What's the scramble, Boss?"

"Company's coming," Jacobs said. "A lawman, out from town."

"Who, Fowler?" one of them inquired.

"A U.S. marshal, in from Salt Lake City. Nosin' into business with the combination."

"What's the play?" asked Tunney.

"Wait and see what happens. If he's easy, we do nothin'. Have your irons handy, in case I give the word."

They ran to fetch their weapons, mostly coming back with pistols, though he also saw a shotgun and a musket in the mix. Eight guns, including his, and Jacobs reckoned that should be enough to do for any man, Mormon or otherwise.

When they were all arranged, lolling about as if they didn't have a job of work to do, Jacobs resumed his vantage point and saw the lawman had advanced to something like a hundred yards from shouting range. Spitting a stream of brown tobacco juice, Jacobs reached back to check the Smith & Wesson Model 1 tucked under his belt, against his spine. It was a tip-up model, just a .22, but loaded seven rimfire cartridges and could be deadly at close range.

Rockwell was closer now. Jacobs could see his long hair underneath a wide-brimmed hat, the matching beard, his buckskin shirt and trousers. Big Sharps rifle propped across his saddle, two Colt Navy pistols—and was that a *tomahawk* stuck through his belt?

"Marshal," he called out, when his enemy had closed to thirty yards. "What can I do for you?"

"Just some questions that I need to ask you," Rockwell answered, as he moved in closer, counting seven other men behind the one he took for Emil Jacobs. Maybe they were done with digging for the day, but was it likely all of them would carry guns into the mine?

"What kinda questions?" Jacobs wondered.

Rockwell had already cocked the Sharps, and had his index finger on its trigger as he answered back, "About the Murphy brothers' claim."

"Murphy?"

"Your mayor says you're the man to see."

"Did he." Not making it a question.

"Seemed to think you could enlighten me about whatever happened to the former owners."

"Those would be the Mormons."

"Would be. Yes."

"And Beardsley sent you here."

"Since you and he are both investors in the mine."

"Uh-huh."

"So, what about it?"

"Don't know what to tell ya, Marshal. Paul's the one who tipped me they were sellin' out. I put some money in the pot, along with him and Isaac Walton. Mormons left, Murphys moved in."

"My question would be *where* they went."

Jacobs leaned forward, spat tobacco juice, then straightened up again, his right hand drifting slowly back behind his hip. A gun back there, Rockwell assumed, watching the others tensing up.

"I couldn't say exac'ly where they are, right now, but if you wanna meet 'em—"

Rockwell drilled him with the Sharps, dead-center, just as Jacobs reached his hideout gun, then dropped the rifle, rolling through a dismount on the Appaloosa's right-hand side and clearing both his Colts, before he landed in a crouch, swinging the pistol in his left hand to propel the horse out of his way.

The miners had not been prepared to see their boss cut down, turning the snow red where he fell. And they weren't ready for what happened next, either. Rockwell fired twice, one Colt and then the other, taking down the adversaries who were holding long guns, still in shock from seeing Jacobs drop. He hit one in the upper chest, the other just above his belt buckle. The first one dropped his musket as he toppled over, but the other fired a shotgun blast that cut a third man's legs from under him and left him thrashing on the ground.

A bonus.

The four still on their feet were breaking off to either side of Rockwell, clawing six-guns from their belts, no holsters. Rockwell swiveled to his right and clipped one on the run, blood spurting from the miner's neck to mark the point of impact. With a pivot to the left, he caught another of the miners lining up a shot and beat him to it, point and squeeze, not focusing on the result as long as there were others left to face.

The last two had their guns in hand, firing at Rockwell without taking time to aim. The fear of dying made them sloppy and became a self-fulfilling prophecy. Rockwell steadied his right-hand Colt and plugged a bullet through the nearest shooter's rib cage, spinning him around to fall facedown with arms outflung.

The last one bolted for the mine shaft, firing blindly back over his shoulder. Rockwell saw him disappear into the darkness there and thought about pursuing him, then spied an open case of dynamite resting beside the tunnel's mouth. He walked across to it, retrieved a stick already fitted with a fuse, and struck a match to set it sputtering. When half its length had burned away, he pitched it down into the shaft and backed off, waiting for the blast, the sound of falling rock, and the eruption of a choking dust cloud from the mine.

Surveying what was left, he found two of the miners still alive, if only just. Rockwell picked up their guns and tossed them out of reach before he went to fetch his Sharps, then whistled up his Appaloosa for the ride back into Tartarus.

"So, what's the plan?" Brett Murphy asked.

Paul Beardsley faced the brothers from behind his desk, inside his office at the Lucky Strike.

Brett had a worried air about him. Clem, by contrast, simply seemed to be confused.

"I sent him out to Emil's place," said Beardsley, "hoping he'll take care of it."

"And if he don't?" asked Brett.

"Then it comes back to us."

"Can't say I like the sound of that," Brett said. "This Rockwell's s'pose to be a tough one."

"Well, there's always the alternative."

"How's that?"

"You could surrender."

"Hey, now," Clem chipped in for the first time.

"Something to think about," said Beardsley. "You could just confess and make it easy all around."

"Confess to what, exactly?" Brett demanded.

"Start with murder of the Mormons. Then, there's claim-jumping. They'll likely call that robbery."

"We sure as hell ain't doin' that," Clem said.

"And if we did," Brett added, "you'd be goin' down along with us. The judge, too."

"Would we?"

"How you figger otherwise?" Brett challenged him.

"The town's mayor and a justice of the peace," said Beardsley. "Our word, stacked against the two of you. Who do you think a jury will believe?"

"You're forgettin' ever'body else in town who knows about it," Brett replied.

"Oh, sure. They'll all be lining up to hang themselves for your sake, will they?"

"Brett?" Clem sounded worried now.

"Shut up!" To Beardsley, then: "If Rockwell gets past Jacobs and his men, you know damn well the two of us can't take him on our own."

"You won't be on your own," Beardsley replied. "My boys'll help you out."

"Well, hey. You coulda said that in the first place."

"And you may not have to deal with him at all. There's something else, though."

"What would that be?"

"Say that Emil takes him. There's a chance he could be mad about me sending Rockwell out his way."

"You think?"

"It's possible. He lets his temper get the best of him, sometimes."

"So, talk him out of it," Brett said.

"I'll try, o'course. But if I can't . . ."

"Don't tell me."

"When you think about it, what's one more?"

"And all his boys," said Clem.

"Hirelings. They'll fight if Emil tells 'em to, but if he's gone, who foots the bill?"

"You take a lot for granted," Brett observed.

"Somebody in my business needs the knack of reading human nature."

"Uh-huh. What's that readin' tell you about me and Clem?"

Instead of calling them a pair of stupid louts, Beardsley replied, "I'd say you're men who want to get ahead in life, no matter what it takes. You see something you want and grab it."

"Mebbe so." Brett smiled. "Mebbe that's just exac'ly right."

Approaching Tartarus, Rockwell rode wide around the town's north end and came back to the livery from its east side, taking the hostler by surprise. Rockwell instructed him to leave the Appaloosa saddled, while providing feed and water. "Someone comes in asking questions," he advised, "just say I dropped the horse off and you don't know where I went."

"Tell 'em the truth, in other words," the hostler answered, with a gap-toothed grin.

"And if there's trouble, be prepared to get the horses out, quick as you can."

"Sounds like you're countin' on it, Marshal."

"Let's just say I wouldn't be surprised."

Rockwell went out the same way he had entered, through the back, and walked along behind the shops on Main Street's eastern side, trailing a lye soap odor to the Chinese laundry. As before, he found a number of Celestials clustered around the back door, cooling off, a couple of them smoking bamboo pipes loaded with something that smelled sweeter than tobacco. As he neared them, one ducked back inside the laundry and returned a moment later with the old man who had talked to Rockwell earlier. This time, the elder stood and stared, unspeaking, eyeing the big Sharps cradled in Rockwell's arms.

"You helped me earlier," said Rockwell. "I appreciate it, and I wanted to advise you that I have some work to do in town."

"Killing," the old man said.

"Most likely. None of it's to do with you, but people being what they are, I reckon you deserve a warning."

"Should we pack and leave?"

"I won't say that, just yet. You know the townsfolk here better than I do. If it goes against me, do whatever's necessary to protect your people."

The old man said something to the others in Chinese, a couple of them asking questions. When he'd hushed them, he asked Rockwell, "Will you burn the town?"

"I thought about it, but I don't like being wasteful. There's some people waiting for me. One way or another, you'll be rid of them. I can't say that whoever takes their place will be a big improvement."

"More white men."

"Way of the world," Rockwell allowed. "This world, at least."

"We cannot help you, Marshal."

"Wouldn't ask you to," Rockwell replied. "Just wanted you to have a fighting chance if anything goes wrong."

It felt a bit like blasphemy, suggesting that he might be vulnerable to his foes despite the Prophet's blessing, but he didn't think the old Celestial would buy that angle anyhow. Rockwell did not intend to die in Tartarus, but there was such a thing as tempting Fate with over-confidence that verged on sinful pride.

Leaving the elder and his people to whatever preparations they might make, he backtracked to the alley where he'd helped the Chinese girl and angled back toward Main Street. Rockwell had planned his order of attack while he was riding back to Tartarus, leaving the carnage at the Silver Beauty mine. He knew Chief Fowler must be neck-deep in the town's corruption, but he had to give the lawman one last chance.

For what? Maybe redemption, though it didn't fall under the jurisdiction of the U.S. Marshals Service. He would see the chief and let him pick a side, already knowing how the call would likely go. And when he'd made that effort, then it would be time to deal with Beardsley, Walton, and whoever else thought it would be a good idea to back their move on Judgment Day.

Emerging onto Main Street, Rockwell looked both ways and saw no one who seemed to be on watch for him, particularly. There were people going in and out of shops as usual, some loitering in front of the saloons, but nothing in the way of sentries. As for Main Street's windows, Rockwell couldn't say who might be peering through them, waiting for a shot at him, but he was bound to cross the street regardless, come what may.

He didn't dawdle, passed directly from the alley that concealed him to the sidewalk opposite, then turned left toward the door labeled POLICE, between the Gold Dust and the Lucky Strike. Fowler had called himself the chief, but Rockwell had not seen another badge in town so far, besides his own. He guessed that deputies might be recruited as the need arose, without maintaining any kind of standing force.

Better for him. He'd likely only have to kill one crooked lawman, then get down to business with the mayor, the justice of the peace, and whoever they used to do their dirty work. The whole town, maybe, if it came to that.

Whatever happened, Rockwell had a debt to settle, for his nephew and the other murdered Saints.

And he would likely have to settle it with blood.

He didn't knock on Fowler's door, just barged on in and found the chief seated behind his desk, a whiskey bottle and a half-filled glass standing in front of him. Fowler looked up, not startled. "So, you're back," he said.

"Looks like it."

"Talk to Emil Jacobs, did you?"

"Briefly."

"Was the conversation fruitful?"

"Dragged a little, toward the end."

"And now he's dead, I guess?"

"Got jumpy," Rockwell said. "I had to settle him."

"And how'd his men take that?"

"They're settled, too."

"Which brings you back to Tartarus."

"It had to happen."

"I suppose." Fowler rose slowly, wincing as if something pained him. "I'm supposed to be the law here."

"Why I'm talking to you," Rockwell said. "See if you'll help me clean this up."

"And how'm I s'pose to do that, when I made the mess to start with?"

"I don't figure you planned any of it, Chief."

"I didn't stop it, either. Didn't lift a finger, afterward, to punish anyone."

"There's still time."

"No, there ain't. I'm done, and we both know it."

"Want to lock yourself inside that cell?"

"And hang a month from now, in Salt Lake City? Hell, no. Let's just get 'er done."

133

Rockwell shifted the Sharps to his left hand, freeing his right. "Your call."

Fowler was breathing like a man stoking a bellows, working up his nerve, cheeks going blotchy from the effort. When his slack hand rose to clutch at the revolver on his hip, Rockwell was ready with his Colt, blasting a vent in Fowler's chest from ten feet out. The bullet's impact pitched his target back against the wall where WANTED circulars were tacked. Some of the posters came down with him as he slithered to the floor, leaving some others smeared with gore.

Rockwell stood over Fowler as he breathed his last, then helped himself to the chief's revolver. It was an old Colt Paterson, out of production for ten years or more, but still serviceable. He checked it over, found its five-shot cylinder fully loaded with .36-caliber rounds, and tucked the pistol underneath his belt, around in back.

Facing a force of unknown size, you couldn't have too many guns.

Leaving the chief for someone else to cart away, Rockwell went out and left the door open behind him, seeking other enemies.

CHAPTER 11

"You hear a shot?" Brett Muphy asked his brother Clem.

"I mighta."

"Sound like it came from the chief's office?"

"Dunno."

"What *do* you know?"

Clem grinned at him, raising his glass. "This ain't the best whiskey I ever drunk."

"Idjit!"

"Hey, now!"

"Shut up. One of us needs to go and see if somethin' happened with the chief."

"I'll wait right here," Clem said, his free hand resting on the Colt Walker he'd slipped inside the waistband of his trousers.

"Hell you will. We'll flip for it," Brett told him, fishing in his pocket for a coin.

"Uh-oh."

Brett glanced up at his brother, saw him staring at the barroom's bat-wing doors, and turned in that direction, just as Porter Rockwell stepped into the Lucky Strike. The long-haired, bearded marshal held his big Sharps rifle in his left hand, so the right was free to go for either of his Navy Colts.

I guess we know what happened to the chief,

Brett thought, his stomach twisting up into a knot.

Brett was behind the bar, his brother out in front of it, a little act they'd come up with together after Beardsley ordered them to guard the Lucky Strike. There was a sawed-off double-barreled shotgun on a shelf in front of him, about waist-high, already cocked, but he was suddenly afraid to reach for it.

"I'm looking for the mayor," said Rockwell, moving slowly toward them. There were only half a dozen drinkers in the place, and most of them were leaving now, as fast as they could travel without prodding Rockwell into shooting one of them. Meanwhile, the lawman's eyes were locked on Brett and Clem.

They weren't alone, of course. Beardsley had Mickey Shaughnessy hiding in back, waiting to help them out, and Brett wished he would hurry up about it. Started wondering if maybe he'd skedaddled out the back door when the boss left, on his way to visit Isaac Walton. Bunch of yellow bellies he'd been stuck with—and his brother, who was twitching now, to beat the band.

"He ain't here," Brett told Rockwell. "Maybe try another time."

"You don't mind if I have a look in back," the marshal said, not asking. "Just to satisfy myself."

"Can't letcha do that," Clem advised him,

with the whiskey talking. Brett wished he could slap his brother, but he started reaching for the scattergun, instead.

"You of a mind to stop me, then?" asked Rockwell, closer now and watching both of them.

"I am," Clem said, and made his last mistake, trying to pull his Colt.

Rockwell was faster. Lord, the speed on him! He shot Clem once, then swung his piece toward Brett, but didn't waste a shot as Brett dropped down behind the bar. About that time, Mickey arrived, banging away at Rockwell, crying out as the marshal returned fire and drilled him. Brett was cringing, still trying to reach the shotgun, when a stray shot hit one of the lamps behind the bar and it exploded, raining fire.

He scrabbled down the shotgun from its shelf and used it as a crutch to raise himself, his boots on fire, flames licking at his trouser cuffs and biting at his ankles. Sobbing from the pain and for his brother, Murphy swung the stubby gun around toward Rockwell, but the marshal had him spotted, squeezing off a shot that drove a spike of agony between his ribs. Falling, Brett squeezed the shotgun's double triggers, shattering a dozen whiskey bottles shelved behind the bar, their alcoholic contents spewing out to feed the fire surrounding him.

He wasn't sure if Rockwell, headed for the office, even heard him scream.

• • •

Rockwell didn't bother knocking on the office door. He kicked it in and followed through behind his Colt, three chambers empty now. There was nobody at the mayor's desk to greet him, no one hiding in the closet when he checked it, making sure.

So, if the Murphy boy had spoken truthfully, where should he look for Beardsley next? Someplace where he felt safe, with men and guns around him, if he hadn't already cleared out of Tartarus.

Not yet, he thought. The boss would want to stick around and deal with Rockwell if he could. Beardsley owned too much property to simply pull up stakes and run out at a moment's notice. There'd be money to collect from his establishments, and likely from the bank. Supplies to gather if he had a trip in mind.

Rockwell knew Beardsley owned two more saloons, the Nugget and the Mother Lode. He could be hiding out at either one of them, or at his residence, wherever that was. Maybe with his partner, Isaac Walton, at the office where he did his bit as justice of the peace. In fact, he might wind up searching the town from end to end.

Better get started, then.

Retreating to the barroom, Rockwell moved through smoke that made his eyes tear up, passing the men he'd shot. He figured that Brett Murphy must be down behind the bar, burned up by now, with bright flames spreading up the whiskey wall and leaping to the rafters. It would take a miracle to save the Lucky Strike, and Rockwell guessed that miracles were something rarely seen in Tartarus.

Smoke followed him outside, where he turned back past Fowler's silent office toward the Mother Lode, a half block farther north. He'd passed it by the first time, hoping to catch Beardsley in the office where it seemed he spent most of his time, but now he had to backtrack, searching out his quarry.

By the time he reached the Mother Lode saloon, a cry of "Fire!" had echoed through the town. People were spilling out of shops and offices along Main Street, some of them rallying to form a hasty fire brigade. Buckets appeared from somewhere and were dipped into horse troughs, carried by some brave souls through the smoky doorway of the Lucky Strike. The bucket-bearers came out coughing, telling others on the street to clear the buildings either side of Beardsley's palace.

One of them ducked into Fowler's office and was back a second later, shouting out to no one in particular, "The chief's been shot! He's dead!"

Rockwell ignored the hubbub, waited for a dozen men or so to clear the Mother Lode, then pushed in through its swinging doors. The bartender was on his own, glaring at Rockwell from behind the stick.

"I'm looking for your boss," said Rockwell.

"Haven't seen him."

"Ever?"

"Lately."

"Does he keep an office here?"

"It's private."

"Shouldn't you be out fighting the fire?"

"Ain't my job."

"I'm bound to check that office. Point me to it."

"Point ya straight to Hell," the barkeep said, hunching his shoulders as he reached beneath the bar.

It was an easy shot from ten feet, through his left eye, pieces of the bullet or his skull cracking a mirror mounted on the wall behind the ranks of bottles. Two rounds still remaining in the Navy Colt as Rockwell walked around the far end of the bar and through a beaded curtain, to another door marked PRIVATE.

No one home.

Before he left, he swapped the Colt's near-empty cylinder for one with all six chambers loaded. Kept the pistol in his right hand as he stepped onto the sidewalk, glancing back in the direction of the Lucky Strike, where smoke was pouring from the upstairs windows now. He saw more of it seeping out through shingles on the roof of Fowler's former office, as the fire began to spread.

One more saloon to check, before he started going door to door, and Rockwell wondered how much of the town would still be standing when he started on his rounds.

"We can't just *sit* here," Isaac Walton said, his whiny tone grating on Beardsley's nerves.

"You want to go out in the street and face him, then?" asked Beardsley.

"You're supposed to have that covered," said the justice of the peace.

"It *is* covered. Just give my people time."

"For what? To let him burn the town around us?"

"Hold your water, will you?" Beardsley sneered. "I'd guess he took the Murphys by surprise, is all."

"The world's been taking those two by surprise since they were born."

"It's impolite to speak ill of the dead," said Beardsley.

"Impolite?" Walton produced a huffing noise. "I want to know how we're supposed to get clear of this mess."

"Once Rockwell's dealt with, we pack up and go."

"Start over, somewhere else?"

"Unless you'd rather wait around and hang."

"Goddamn it, Paul!"

"We always knew this day would come."

"*Might* come, not *would*. If I'd known it was guaranteed—"

"What? You'd have turned the silver profits down? Pitched in to help the Mormons?"

Walton made no response to that, but reached out for his whiskey glass.

"I didn't think so," Beardsley said. "We're in this thing together, and that's how we're getting out of it."

"All right," the judge replied. "What now?"

Beardsley withdrew a pistol from his desk drawer, sliding it across toward Walton. "First, protect yourself."

Staring at the weapon, Walton said, "I'm not a gunman."

"Be a *man,* at least."

"Is this the measure of it?"

"I would say it is, today."

Reluctantly, Walton picked up the pistol, hefting it. He thumbed the hammer back to half-cock, spun the cylinder, then lowered it again. "All right. What next?"

"Collect whatever money you can get your hands on in a hurry, and come straight back here. We'll see the marshal taken care off, then go by the bank on our way out of town and get the rest."

"Herb won't like it."

Picturing the chubby, balding banker, Beardsley

said, "Who cares what Herbie Sims likes? He's a fatter man today, because of us."

"I'd better go." Walton stood up, tried shoving the pistol into his waistband, then gave it up and held the weapon loosely in his hand. "See you."

"Buck up," Beardsley advised. "A few hours from now, we'll be new men."

Nodding, the judge went out and shut the office door behind him. Beardsley let his smile relax into a brooding frown. Walton was clearly approaching the end of his rope, slipping into depression and guilt. Handing him a loaded six-gun was a gamble, but if he decided it was easier to use it on himself, so what? That simply meant another problem solved, more cash for Beardsley in the end.

It wasn't what he'd had in mind at first, when he'd decided they should jump the Mormon claim, but crying over spilt milk was a waste of time. The only thing Beardsley regretted, truth be told, was getting caught.

That hadn't happened yet, though.

Porter Rockwell still had trials to face before he got to Beardsley and the end of it in Tartarus.

A full half block of Main Street was engulfed in wind-whipped flames when Rockwell walked into the Nugget. He had reloaded the Sharps and the spare Colt cylinder, working quickly in an alley while he watched the panic spread through town. Fire was the worst thing that could happen to a rural settlement, aside from plague, made worse in desert towns by water shortages. He reckoned that the western half of Tartarus was doomed already, and the eastern half's survival would depend in large part on the wind's direction as the afternoon wore on.

But Rockwell was not waiting for the fire to do his job. He still had guilty souls to ferret out and punish with his own two hands.

Thy will be done.

At first, he thought the Nugget was deserted, then he heard a whistle. Two figures rose behind the bar, while two more came from somewhere to his left and overhead, moving across a kind of balcony that overlooked the barroom from the second floor. The two behind the bar had shotguns, while the pair upstairs made do with pistols.

Rockwell did not bother asking whether Beardsley was around. Before the shooters had a chance to open up, he threw himself to one side of the bat-wing doors and tipped a table over on its side, facing the bar, to use as cover. It was oak, he thought, but didn't stand much of a chance against the buckshot ripping through it with a sound like thunder, as the double-barrels both let go together. Splinters stung him, but the pellets missed, and Rockwell took advantage of the time the pair with scatterguns were bound to take reloading.

Rising from behind the shattered table, Colt in hand, he shot the taller of the two men on the balcony, watching a spout of blood erupt from where the bullet scored his throat. It was a killing wound, though not immediately fatal, but the wounded man went down and Rockwell heard his pistol clatter on the balcony.

He and the second upstairs shooter fired together, bullets crossing in midair. The gunman's slug whistled within an inch or two of Rockwell's ear, then he was doubled over, gut-shot, tumbling in an awkward somersault over the rail and plummeting to land behind the bar. The cursing that erupted there told Rockwell that he must have fallen onto one of the two shooters trying to reload.

Rockwell switched weapons, raised the Sharps and sighted roughly on the cursing voice behind the bar. It bucked against his shoulder as he squeezed the trigger, its .52-caliber slug punching through the bar's front paneling, and the profanity was cut short by a howl of pain.

He had the Sharps reloaded with another paper cartridge when the second barman rose, his double-barrel swinging toward its target. Rockwell got there first, another crack of smoky thunder from his rifle, and the scatter-gunner's head exploded like a gourd with fireworks packed inside.

Rockwell got up and palmed his Colt, crossing to move around the bar. His rifle slug had crushed the hidden shooter's hip and left him wallowing in blood, shotgun forgotten, as he clutched himself and moaned.

"Where's Beardsley?" Rockwell asked him.

"Gone. Knew you were coming."

"*Where,* not *why.*"

"Dunno. Oh God, it hurts!"

Rockwell considered finishing his misery, then saved a slug and left him to it. Half of Tartarus would soon be ashes, maybe taking Beardsley with it, but he couldn't leave that part to chance. As long as any part remained, the hunt went on.

Where next? The judge's office, maybe . . . or the house where money lived.

Walton was already inside the bank with Herbert Sims, the president and manager, when Beardsley entered with an empty leather satchel in his hand. The whole place smelled of smoke, though it was on the east side of Main Street and safe, so far. Sims displayed a sickly pallor, whether from the town's advancing immolation or the judge's large withdrawal from the vault, Beardsley could not have said.

"You too," the banker said, at sight of Beardsley. "I suppose I should've known."

"Nothing's forever, Herb," Beardsley replied.

In a stricken voice, Sims said, "The town. We were supposed to grow and prosper. You remember that?"

"Luck of the draw," said Beardsley. "Are you ready, Isaac?"

"As I'll ever be," said Walton, gray faced, sounding nearly as depressed as Sims.

"Christ, you two are gloomy. Try to see the opportunity in this."

"What opportunity?" Sims challenged him.

"To start fresh," Beardsley said. "New territory and new people. Hell, a whole new life."

"A new life?" Sims stared back at him, incredulous. "I'm forty-two years old, for heaven's sake!"

Beardsley considered that, then pictured Sims turning against him, under pressure from the law, making a deal to testify and thereby save himself.

"I guess you're right," said Beardsley, as he drew his pistol, a .31-caliber Remington Beals pocket revolver, and shot Sims in the face.

Walton lurched backward as the banker fell, crying, "My God!"

"He had nothing to do with it," Beardsley replied.

"But why? Why Herb?"

"He was a weakling. Think about it, Isaac? How long do you think he'd hold out when the law came asking questions?"

"Still."

"Still, *what?*"

"It's so . . . cold blooded."

"Worse than killing Mormons?" Beardsley sneered, "or is it just because you saw it done this time?"

"It's just . . . I didn't see it going on and on like this."

"Well, Christ all Friday, Isaac."

Looking at another weak link in the chain, Paul Beardsley raised his Remington and blew a hole in Walton's chest. The judge went down, wriggling and gasping like a man trying to rise out of a fever dream. Beardsley stood over him and fired another shot into his forehead, ending it. That done, he put away his pocket pistol and retrieved the gun he loaned to Walton earlier, tucking it underneath his belt. He picked up Walton's satchel, too, before the spreading pool of blood could stain it. With his empty bag, he carried it around the cashier's counter, to the open vault in back.

There was no reason why the cash should go to waste. There was no question he had earned his share, and why not just take all of it—or, anyway, as much as he could carry.

Looking out at Tartarus in flames, he reckoned that the town had little need of money now.

CHAPTER 12

Main Street was blowing up a storm. The desert wind that had initially fanned flames along the avenue's west side had given way to something else, a draft from Hell's own bellows, making Rockwell sweat as he walked down the middle of the street. Around him, he identified two different kinds of citizens: those who already had been burned out of their shops and homes, watching the flames with ghastly faces, and the others who'd been spared so far but didn't know how long their luck would hold.

He felt some of them staring at him as he passed among them, three Colts in his belt, the big Sharps cradled in his arms. He saw the fear and hatred in their eyes, but no one made a move against him. They were frightened, more than furious, afraid to lose their lives on top of all their worldly goods.

Rockwell could muster nothing in the way of pity for them. He would never know how many of them were aware of what had happened to the murdered Saints. And frankly, he no longer cared. He had identified the men behind the killings, and had dealt with all but two of them, unless they had more flunkies posted somewhere on the safe side of the street, waiting to snipe at him.

149

Isaac Walton's office had gone up in smoke before he reached it, leaving nothing for him but the bank. Still standing, opposite the fiery ruin of the Mother Lode saloon, its door was shut and had a CLOSED sign hanging on the inside of the upper half, made out of glass. Rockwell supposed they had no fear of someone breaking in, before today.

He tried the doorknob, and it turned. Taking a cautious step inside, he saw two bodies stretched out on the floor in front of him. One man, shot through the left cheek by his nose, he didn't recognize. Likely a bank employee, possibly the man in charge. The other, also strange to Rockwell, had been shot once in the chest, and then again, above his left eyebrow. A gold medallion dangling from the watch chain on his vest was etched with three small letters.

I.M.W.

For Isaac Something Walton?

Probably, and that left only one man to be hunted down.

Before he left the bank, Rockwell walked back to check the vault and found no one concealed there. Sacks of what he took for coins, and maybe silver nuggets, lined a set of shelves, but he could find no paper currency. Add robbery and two more murders to the list of Beardsley's crimes.

Leaving the vault, he spied a back door standing open and went out that way, peering in both directions, hoping for a glimpse of Beardsley. There was no sign of him, certainly no point in studying the arid, sandy soil for footprints that would give a clue to his chosen direction.

Never mind.

If he was leaving Tartarus, he needed transportation.

Which meant he was heading for the livery.

"Saddle my bay," Beardsley commanded, getting edgy when the hostler stood and stared at him. "Right now!"

"Yessir."

The old man shuffled off to do his bidding, Beardsley chafing at his sluggishness and wishing he could beat some youth into the man. Cursing, he retreated to the open door fronting on Main Street, leaning out to watch the town die, scanning faces on the street in search of Porter Rockwell's.

Damn the man! Why did he have to come along on his crusade and ruin everything?

He and his fellow marshals hadn't managed to arrest the Mountain Meadows murderers, who'd killed ten times the number slain in Tartarus, but maybe that was by design. If Beardsley had disposed of people Rockwell and his church called Gentiles, would the marshal even care?

It made no difference now, of course. The damage had been done.

He turned back toward the hostler, shouting, "Are you finished yet?"

"Comin' right up!"

"Be quick about it!"

It was risky, hurrying the old fool, but his nerves demanded action. Beardsley knew he'd have to check the cinch straps, make sure they were tight enough to keep his saddle on the bay before he galloped off and got dumped on his butt within a mile of town.

There'd been no time to count his money while he was collecting it in haste, but Beardsley had a decent head for figures. He'd been thirty-seven thousand dollars to the good before he picked up Isaac Walton's share, plus whatever was left inside the vault at Herbie's bank. Enough to settle anywhere, rebuild his life under a new name and live happily until the Reaper came to visit, in another forty years or so.

Whatever it came out to, finally, Beardsley regarded it as no more than his due. The whole town owed him for the hard work he'd put into it, and now that he was forced to flee, he saw a certain justice in the fact that so little of Tartarus would be left standing in his absence.

"Better luck next time," he muttered to the flaming ruins on the western side of Main Street.

Now he heard the hostler coming with his bay mare, moving slower than molasses on a winter morning. Beardsley went to meet him, set his satchels down while he was checking on the saddle cinches, then considered what to do with them once he was mounted.

Yet another damned delay.

"Do you have any good strong twine?" he asked the hostler.

"Should have."

"Well? Go fetch it!"

"Yessir."

The old man picked up his pace a little as he headed for a work bench, coming back a moment later with a ball of braided sisal string. He handed it to Beardsley, watching while his anxious customer measured a double length and cut it with a pocket knife, then tied it to the handles of his two fat leather bags. It was a pleasant strain to hoist them, twisting string around the saddle horn, so that one satchel hung on either side.

Ready at last.

Beardsley shoved several coins into the hostler's hand, not bothering to count them as he climbed aboard the bay. Without a backward glance, he spurred the animal and galloped past the stable's open doors.

Rockwell had circled back to Main Street on his way to reach the stable, watching out for Beardsley as he went, in case he had misjudged the man somehow. It made sense for his quarry to escape, but manhunting had taught him that a character who's desperate might not be thinking sensibly. He'd seen men stand and fight when they were sure to lose, and others run when they could probably have saved themselves if they'd had grit enough to try.

There must have been two hundred people on the street by now, watching the fire and basking in its heat. A couple of them grumbled something as he passed, but Rockwell didn't catch it and he didn't care, unless one of them made a move against him. As it happened, none of them was brave or dumb enough to try him. Nor were any of them armed, from what he saw so far.

That part could change, he realized. It only took one loud-mouthed, angry person to arouse a mob, and he could have real trouble on his hands. But looking at the people lining Main Street's eastern sidewalk, Rockwell thought they looked defeated, beaten down. Maybe *resigned?* He wondered if their shared guilt had prepared them for a day like this, when everything they'd built would lie in ashes at their feet.

Nearing the laundry, Rockwell saw the Chinese moving out. Their shacks were on the safe side of the street, at least for now, but they weren't taking any chances. They had packed two wagons, hitching them to mules he hadn't seen before, not waiting for the wind to shift and turn the flames or round-eyed populace against them.

From his seat of honor in the lead wagon, the old man stared at Rockwell, might have nodded to him, but the drifting smoke left that in doubt.

Rockwell was fifty yards out from the livery when Beardsley, mounted, suddenly appeared, hunched over in his saddle, riding hell-bent for the northern end of Tartarus and anything that lay beyond it. Stopping in his tracks, Rockwell shouldered the Sharps and framed his target in its sights.

One chance, and Beardsley would be out of range for decent shooting by the time he could reload. That meant a chase, maybe for miles, and Rockwell thought he'd rather end it here, if possible. He took a breath and held it, gently squeezed the trigger, waiting for the heavy kick against his shoulder when the hammer fell.

There was a heartbeat when he thought he might have missed, then Beardsley arched his back, one arm outflung, the other maybe clutching at his saddle horn. Then he was falling, taking something with him as he tumbled and the bay ran on without him. Saddlebags, perhaps, one of them bursting open when it hit the ground, loosing a storm of paper scraps.

Advancing, Rockwell saw that it was currency, wind-whipped, some of it being sucked into the nearby wall of flames. He watched a final tremor run through Beardsley's frame before the man lay still, his jacket, vest, the shirt beneath it sodden crimson where the big Sharps slug had come out through his rib cage.

It appeared that he had tried to take the money with him, even dying. As it was, his left hand clutched a length of twine he'd tied between the two black satchels, so that they had dropped on either side of him, the left one springing open on impact. Rockwell knelt down to close it, then released the death grip while he could, before the fingers started stiffening. He hoisted both satchels by the twine connecting them and backtracked toward the stable where he'd left his Appaloosa.

"Didn't get far," said the hostler, eyeing Beardsley's corpse.

"They rarely do."

"What happens now?"

"Depends on what the fire leaves, and what people want to do with it," Rockwell replied.

"It's burning out," the old man said. "I reckon we're okay."

"You think so?"

"Feel the wind. It's shifting."

"I hadn't noticed."

"Maybe 'cause you ain't from here. I'll get your horse."

When he returned, Rockwell gave him a bundle he'd removed from one of Beardsley's bags, not counting it. The old man blinked and frowned. "You paid up in advance," he said.

"A little something extra. Just in case."

"Well . . ."

Rockwell mounted, slung the bags across the saddle horn in front of him as Beardsley had. "Take care," he told the old man.

"*Adiós*."

The old man had it right, he realized. The wind *had* shifted. It was at his back as Rockwell started out of Tartarus, or what remained of it. Lord willing, it would hasten him along to Salt Lake City, sparing him from snow until he had a roof over his head.

And after that?

He faced the future grim-faced, stoic. Thinking to himself, *Thy will be done.*

ABOUT THE AUTHOR

Michael Newton has published 282 books since 1977. His work includes 200 novels (published under his own name and various pen names), plus 82 nonfiction books in the fields of true crime, history and cryptozoology. His history of the Florida Ku Klux Klan (*The Invisible Empire*, University Press of Florida) won the Florida Historical Society's Rembert Patrick Award as Best Book in Florida History for 2002. In 2006 the American Library Association chose his *Encyclopedia of Cryptozoology* (McFarland Publishing) as one of the year's 12 Outstanding Reference Books. His novel *Manhunt* (written as "Lyle Brandt" for Berkley Books) won the Western Fictioneers Peacemaker Award for Best Western Novel in 2010. Newton lives in Indiana with his wife, Heather. Visit him on Facebook or through his Web site at www.michaelnewton.homestead.com.

Center Point Large Print
600 Brooks Road / PO Box 1
Thorndike, ME 04986-0001 USA

(207) 568-3717

US & Canada:
1 800 929-9108
www.centerpointlargeprint.com